# THE LIFE AND TIMES OF BANKA HARICHANDAN

# THE LIFE AND TIMES OF BANKA HARICHANDAN

Dipti R. Pattanaik

Translated by Himansu S. Mohapatra

SIMON & SCHUSTER

YODAPRESS

London · New York · Sydney · Toronto · New Delhi

First published in India by Simon & Schuster India and Yoda Press, 2023

1 3 5 7 9 10 8 6 4 2

Simon & Schuster India
818, Indraprakash Building,
21, Barakhamba Road,
New Delhi 110001.
www.simonandschuster.co.in

Yoda Press
79 Gulmohar Enclave
New Delhi 110049
www.yodapress.co.in

Paperback ISBN: 9789392099991
eBook ISBN: 9789392099977
Typeset in India by SŪRYA, New Delhi
Printed and bound in India by Replika Press Pvt. Ltd.

FSC
www.fsc.org
MIX
Paper from responsible sources
FSC® C016779

Simon & Schuster India is committed to sourcing paper that is made from wood grown in sustainable forests and support the Forest Stewardship Council, the leading international forest certification organisation. Our books displaying the FSC logo are printed on FSC certified paper.

*For*
*Paul St-Pierre*
*Satya P. Mohanty*
*Kerstin W. Shands*

*The first two for their valuable and significant work in showcasing Odia literature in the global arena, and, the last named for her firm belief that Banka Harichandan matters.*

# CONTENTS

# PREFACE

A child lingers in an adult, and for that child the adult seeks to return to their childhood again and again. They know that such a return is impossible; therefore, they try to recreate it in their literature, religion, imagination and memory. The more powerful this tension is in a person, the wider is their consciousness. This tension makes the mundaneness of life more meaningful.

All art is a quest for this greater meaningfulness. Probably, for this reason there is a deep affinity between art and the point of view of a child. A child's worldview is an invitation and a challenge to transcend the ordinary and the quotidian that defines our outward-bound life.

# INTRODUCTION

*Himansu S. Mohapatra*

## A New Leaf Quietly Turned

Sometime around the turn of the twentieth century a short story named "Jatrara Dinalipi" (literally "The Diary of a Trip", translated in this book as 'The Account of a Pilgrimage'), published in the prestigious Odia literary monthly *Jhankara*, made readers and lovers of the modern Odia short story sit up and take notice.

The story set out to describe a day's outing to the temple and seaside town of Puri undertaken by a sixteen-year-old in the company of his friend. The trip started amid much fanfare and anticipation for the boy because it promised some precious hours of freedom from the confines of a spartan home. But it ended excruciatingly frustratingly for him upon his realising that his friend had his own personal agenda in going to Puri and had tricked the boy into tagging along. The trip was an object lesson in self-awareness for the boy besides giving him a much-needed reality check.

The story was narrated in a leisurely fashion and with close attention to the banal minutiae of everyday life in a semi-provincial town that the characters seek to escape, albeit on a small scale, partly with the aid of adventure stories (like *Tom Sawyer*, *Huckleberry Finn* and *Treasure Island*) and partly with the help of the trip itself. With the constant self-questioning of the experiencing, analysing mind of a growing boy thrown in for good measure, the story became easily recognisable as a resonant metaphor of adolescent angst and rebellion. A new boy character had been spawned in Odia fiction in the new millennium, Banka Harichandan. A fresh new page in Odia literature, centred on the child and the young adult, was about to unfold.

## A Coming-of-age Narrative is Born

The writer of the short story, Dipti Ranjan Pattanaik, had been writing in *Jhankara* for more than a decade and by 2001 he had published two volumes of short stories. He was beginning to be recognised as an emerging voice in Odia short fiction. Six years before this, in 1995, he had won the national Katha Award for the best short story of the year. With the short story alluded to above, however, Pattanaik seemed to have turned a new leaf in his career as a writer. He had produced a realistic as well as a psychologically compelling story written from the point of view of an adolescent. And it was not a one-off either. He had published two stories featuring Banka in *Jhankara* before. Perhaps he was quietly embarked on a series of Banka stories. The impact made by this third story must have firmed up his determination to go ahead. The result was that about a decade later, in 2010, a landmark volume called *Sandigdha Shaishaba* (*An Angst-ridden Childhood*), comprising eight stories, saw the light of day.

The Banka stories have been a game changer for the author as well as for Odia literature which has always been deficient in sustained narration of childhood and growing up. The book *Sandigdha Shaishaba* won the writer the Odisha Sahitya Akademi award in 2013. Pattanaik has eight volumes of short stories to his credit today. He has continued to write prolifically and on diverse subjects and themes, but the thread of realistic and psychological exploration of childhood sensations and experiences has continued to run through his writing. Recent years have seen the publication of four more significant Banka stories, making the Banka corpus stand at a respectable dozen.

### From Odia to English: *The Life and Times of Banka Harichandan*

It is this corpus that is presented here in an English translation titled *The Life and Times of Banka Harichandan*. The reason for the translation, if one discounts the obvious reason of staging a significant regional-language work on a pan-Indian, or even international platform, is twofold: one, Banka is an unforgettable child character like Oliver or David or Tom or Huck or Jim or Holden Caulfield or

Apu or Rusty or Phatik Chand or Kabi or Sasank[1], but with a distinct Odishan touch, and, two, the Banka stories, in the way they unfold chronologically and thematically, add up to a remarkable coming-of-age narrative in Odia and Indian literature. One may add a third reason. The volume made up of the twelve short stories about Banka Harichandan is one of the most delicate exemplars of a 'composite novel' that one can encounter in the whole gamut of modern Indian literature. In the preface to *Sandigdha Shaishaba*, Pattanaik said that with its sustained spotlight on Banka from story to story, the series makes itself amenable to be read as a composite novel, adding further that he got the cue to compose such a work from the enigmatic American author J.D. Salinger's own work in this genre, namely *Nine Stories* (1953) and "Seymour: An Introduction" (1959), featuring the Glass children. No doubt, this unique blend of the stand-aloneness of each story and the connectedness of stories across borders is the hallmark of the composite novel.

1. The child characters cited range from the familiar ones from Western literature (Oliver, David, Huck, Jim, and Holden Caulfield) to relatively less familiar and unfamiliar ones from Indian literature in English and Odia literature respectively. Rusty is a creation of Ruskin Bond, while Phatik Chand is a creation of Satyajit Ray. Kabi appears in Odia novelist Ganeswar Mishra's *Sakalara Muhan* (translated as *Face of the Morning*; 1996). Sasank is from Odia writer Kamalakanta Mohapatra's short story collection *Chora* (translated as *Crow and Other Stories*; 2008) and can be said to foreshadow, in a rudimentary form, both the coming-of-age story of Banka and the 'composite novel' format through which it is presented.

There is, in fact, more in common between Pattanaik's Banka and Salinger's Holden Caulfield in *The Catcher in the Rye*, his Glass children, especially Teddy (short for Theodore McArdle), than meets the eye. As will be revealed later in the course of this writing, a two-way traffic exists between the boy from Odisha and India and the boy from America.

There is also the inevitable connection through literary genealogy, to the Irish writer James Joyce, nudging this history of Banka in the direction of a portrait of a writer in the Odishan and Indian context. Not only are two of the twelve short stories in the book explicitly about writing, its meaning and mechanics as well as the mysterious process of the emergence of this "divinity in words" ("Initiation"), the entire volume is in a subtle way about the gradual awakening of Banka to his dimly perceived destiny as a writer, especially the kind of writer whom we can call, following Jhumpa Lahiri, "the interpreter of maladies".[2] This aspect of writing can

---

2. That Pattanaik subscribes to Jhumpa Lahiri's notion of the writer as an analyst of various psychic states of dysfunction is clear from how he views the function of writing in his essay "Why I Write". This is how he puts it, "Art arises from an impulse to verbalize the conflict between two intolerable states of being: a state of non-acceptance and a state of non-action in the face of what we can't either accept or endure" (p. 103; translation mine). The essay is included in Pattanaik's eponymous book of essays, *Mu Kanhiki Lekhe* (*Why I Write*), published in 2012.

be presumed to be autobiographical in that something of Pattanaik's writing philosophy can be said to have percolated down to his creation, Banka.

## A Tribute to and a Record of Childhood

But first things first: *The Life and Times of Banka Harichandan* is a coming-of-age narrative of a boy named Banka Harichandan. The narrative covers a period of ten to twelve years in the life of the young hero, starting from age ten when he is in class five to age seventeen when he is a first-year college student. The first seven stories take place in Cuttack of the late nineteen-sixties and mid nineteen-seventies, and then we veer away to the neighbouring town of Choudwar for the next four stories before returning to Cuttack in the last one. The years are arguably the author's upper primary, high school and college years. In the second story, the setting is a nondescript village not far from Cuttack. And in the penultimate story the scene shifts to Puri, the abode of Lord Jagannath. But the action always either starts off from or returns to Cuttack in the end. Thus the entire action of the composite novel is confined within the narrow compass of a small town and its knowable community, satisfying thereby a psychological craving for a unity of place, a craving we all have while reading fiction. Banka's upbringing takes place in an ordinary lower middle-class household that consists of not only Banka's Yama or Nimrod-like father, and his tender-hearted but overworked, and, hence prone-to-occasional-outbursts, mother, his siblings, the dependent grandparents, and of course, Banka's dependent paternal uncle, the infamous Chacha. It is anything but the modern nuclear family that is the norm today.

A qualification also needs to be made about the place. Although it is Cuttack, the most prominent town of Odisha of that time statistically as well as in public perception, as underscored by many telling Odia anecdotes and proverbs, it is nothing like Calcutta. Besides, the delights and attractions of the town—like cinemas, eateries and sporting events and arenas, tailoring houses—being largely out of reach of the young population in ordinary lower middle-class homes, are either non-existent or are objects of frantic and feverish fantasies. Cuttack appears like a limited provincial town in terms of the amenities it offers to its younger crowd, the school and the neighbourhood fields, gullies and paan shops clearly dominating the stage. For all that, Cuttack is still a dream city, covered in the romantic haze of childhood. The second town to feature in the book is Choudwar, on the fringes of Cuttack. It is a further stripped down semi-provincial locale, with its younger population's horizon shrinking to the measure of school and studies only. There is admittedly an Officer's Club here to which Banka goes to watch a movie once in a while, but as a guest of the son of his father's superior officer. He is never allowed to forget the pecking order of society even in the more democratic space of entertainment. The ambience of the semi-provincial set up sees to that.

Politics impinges on the lives of Banka and other boys and girls, be it in Cuttack or Choudwar, but it is rarely obtrusive. And the only "headline" event the narrative refers to—that too incidentally because its main purpose is to provide a context for an eye infection epidemic called "Jai Bangla"—is the Indo-Pak war of 1971. But the narrative doesn't need to be loudly and overtly political or historical. It doesn't have to be, for the work of political indoctrination of young minds to "grow them up"[3] as docile, opportunistic, conformist, and money, success, and job-pursuing future citizens is done by religion and family. The volume is worth reading especially to gain a keener perception of how religion, politics and economics are absorbed into the textures of daily life.

Religion saturates the details of lower middle-class family life in a typical Odishan town in the form of morning prayer at school and evening prayer at home and the constant invocation of the simian god, Hanuman, of the Hindu pantheon. This is the zeitgeist of the time that seeps, nay floods, into the pages of *The Life and Times of Banka Harichandan*. It is the singular achievement of the author to have secreted a questing and self-questioning boy at the book's centre with the result that the lower middle-class domesticity and religious fervour that seeks to naturalise ideology as truth and reason is

---

3. The use of "grow someone up" in the sense of "bring someone up" is inspired by Arundhati Roy's wording in the dedication to her iconic novel *The God of Small Things* (1997).

rendered explicit and is in the process deconstructed. The innocence that is ascribed to childhood in conventional perception is revealed in Banka's case to be subversive. But it does not cease to remain "innocence" for all that.

Banka is a child, and very much of the Wordsworthian kind whose "heart leaps up" at the sight of a rainbow or at the call of the cuckoo or the golden oriole, and, who is the "father of man". He is not a "miniature adult" of the pre-Wordsworthian rationalist discourse. His story filters out the debased currency of experience, guile, cunning, manipulation and abrasion from the unclouded vision of childhood and its corresponding language of hieroglyphic suggestion. The book is thus a tribute to childhood and a record of the full panoply of its manifestations.

## All-of-a-Twist: Guilt and Fear as Keynote

It is true that the predominant emotions of Banka in the book are fear, guilt, shame, anger, and despair and these are consistent with his being a victim. The opening scene of the opening story "An Inauspicious Day in the Life of Banka Harichandan" strikes the keynote to the entire book, showing how the life of this boy in an average lower middle-class Odia family is all-of-a-twist.[4]

---

4. This expression is meant to underline the parallel between Oliver Twist, the poor workhouse boy, and Banka, the average lower middle-class boy, not so much in their background but in the way their emotional lives unravel as a result of fear and guilt.

Banka wakes up in the dead of the night "with a start". His throat is parched and he has to quench his thirst. But how will he navigate the passage from the cot to the water pitcher in the cook room? There are insurmountable obstacles on the way. He is sleeping in one extremity of the cot close to the wall, and, has to cross carefully over the sleeping bodies of his Nani (elder sister), Chhotu (younger brother) and Chacha (father's younger brother) before he can risk climbing down from the cot on the other side. But he must be mindful of his Jejema (paternal grandmother) lying sprawled on a mattress on the floor. If he wakes anyone of them while crossing over them, and, especially if he makes Jejema howl in pain by inadvertently stepping on her in the darkness, then he will be in a soup, as Chacha would "dig rivers of blood on his back". This picture of the sleeping bodies of siblings huddled together in one bed as well as of physical punishment of the "erring" child—erring from whose point of view?—might seem incredible to present-day Indian readers. But it was a fairly common and widespread practice in the time and place that the book is speaking of.

The point, however, is that this was real and it was accepted as a part of family life in another time and place, without of course being covered in glory for the acceptance. It probably is still prevalent in the poorer pockets of Indian society even today. The father of such a family, especially if he was the breadwinning head, had the supreme authority to discipline and punish his child.

Other close relations, living in the house, also had a share in the disciplining process if they were adults.

The child bore the brunt of a brutal disciplinary regime at home, as a result. He—yes, more often than not it was a male child—was assailed by fear, guilt, anger, shame and despair. In the same measure he felt the stirring of craving and desire as an inevitable part of the process of growing up physically and the socialisation process at school and the street. His mind was a veritable battleground of the forces of thanatos and eros. He was constantly tossed on the stormy sea of moral life, torn between the dos of desire and don'ts of ethics, and thereby forced into a life of subterfuge. One quick example of this double life is Banka's hiding of a detective novel of Kanduri Charan Das inside his history book ("Resolution"). Like any child caught in the act of reading a "bajebahi" (bad book), as the detective novel was labelled in those days, Banka is punished by his father. But a few days after this he makes the shocking discovery about his Chacha—and he doesn't escape a thrashing by Banka's father either—reading even more salacious and sexually explicit books by Mastram on the sly, being thus confirmed about the double standards of seemingly good and responsible adults he has interactions with.

So the only way out of such an oppressive regime was for the child to quickly become an adult. This would also be in sync with the shastras. They recommended affectionate, even pampered, rearing until the age of five, the use of the rod until he was fifteen, and, friendly treatment on his attaining the age of sixteen.[5] The irony was, shastras were cited only to be violated or given short shrift in the way the upbringing of children was actually done in middle-class homes. No wonder Banka is seized with an inordinate longing to grow up fast. It is in the book's final chapter that he enters this coveted age of sixteen. But he must ask for what should have been given to him suo motu. He must assert himself and demand dignified treatment if he must free himself from the cycle of repression, as Banka does in the closing sequence of the book's final story, "On the Edge". Banka's, 'Non serviam', though much subdued compared to Stephen Dedalus's, has the same subversive force.

## Reveries, Desires, Dreams: First Steps towards Freedom

But what must Banka do until he arrives on this golden threshold? As the stories leading up to "On the Edge" show, he must desire much against the counsel not to desire. And he must create his rich inner world through dreaming and desire, if only to perfect his tools of imaginative subversion of the goings on in the adult world which has laid down the rules of engagement. Unsurprisingly, the whole narrative is permeated by Banka's oneiric state, which is of two kinds, reveries and dreams.

5. This is a paraphrase of a famous shloka by Chanakya.

In the first, namely reveries, the alphabet of success that comes to him via the mediation of family, school and society is at first rehearsed thoughtlessly and then pondered over so as to be revised and re-phrased. This is a recurrent pattern in the stories. The story in which it receives a classic representation is "Resolution", being ostensibly focused on prayer, the prime cultural vehicle for transmission of societal values. At first the famous Odia prayer (Oh Compassionate Lord, Wanderer of the Universe) is rehearsed blindly. Then as the story unfolds, the confrontation of the prayer's ideality with reality is staged. The terms of the prayer are then rewritten. This second phase of staging, the deconstructive stage, is the most crucial, as can be seen in the quote below.

> All of them must have sung this prayer in their childhood, "Teach me only this O Lord, I need nothing else, neither men nor money." One was taught to always tell the truth. Then, one was also told to shun riches. Why, then, was everybody running like mad to offices, courts, and other places of work? Why was there so much pressure to study well? Why were people getting married? They were praying one way and acting in another? Were they all telling the truth always, his father, mother, chacha and others? Faka was far better than them. Although a rascal himself, his prayers and his deeds matched. Everybody else was a hypocrite. This prayer was false. So was this the omnipresent, omnipotent and omniscient God? Chacha, Nani, Father, Mother all were liars. Was Mother a liar also? It was not easy to believe that.

The story goes on to not only tell us about Faka's blasphemous parody, but cites it as well. And not just in this story, but in the story "Initiation" too, which is woven around Banka wrestling with the writing of an article for the school magazine. It would be interesting to look at Faka's parody of the sacred lines of the famous prayer that Banka will take his cue from in order to perform his own parodic inversion of it in both the stories.

> O Compassionate Lord, the wanderer of the Universe
> Accept my pleadings to your heart
> Take care of the patch of green in your backyard
> And eat it by cutting it.
> ...
> Teach me only this O Lord,
> Not to want a buxom young lass in my bed.

And then, in "Initiation", the most scandalous parody of all, this time of the lines of the *Bhagabata* by Jagannath Das, the text sacred to all Odias.

> The good and bad sides of a living being
> Can be known at the time of their shagging.

Reveries, then, have this important deconstructive function in the coming-of-age narrative of Banka.

Desire too is an intimate part of growing up and is connected with a new sexual awareness focused on the body. In its manifestation as erotic desire it urges one towards body-based interactions with others outside of the family fold. Accordingly, Banka has his fantasies ignited by a succession of pretty faces, starting from the unnamed girl of chapter four through the named ones (Nibedita, Sangita, Preeti, Pramila and so on) in the chapters that follow. Though they go by different names, they are the embodiment of the stereotypical image of the female as temptress. Thus erotic desire in the narrative so often reinforces the societal values of money, success, marriage and of course straightness. The narrative does, however, fail to give agency to any of the girls or credit them with a modicum of intelligence or self-respect, let alone imagining her as transgressive. The narrative imagination of the author also seems to falter in another area: its portrayal of homoerotic love as deviant and dangerous sexual behaviour is in keeping with the ethos of the times and has the effect of undermining same-sex love.

Dreams, however, are more revealing in their close connection with trauma. In the narrative they have their traditional, Freudian function of opening the 'royal road' to the subconscious. The abuses, the beatings and the humiliation that Banka is subjected to at home and school, but that he cannot process, are condensed into dreams. "Timetable" and "Initiation" feature famous dream sequences, set in the Choudwar days of Banka's schooling where he studied the higher classes of ten and eleven.

The first one from "Timetable" ominously shows Banka as a prisoner in the cage of a zoo minutes before the school finals. The criss-crossing bars of the cage resemble the criss-crossing horizontal and vertical pencil lines of the timetable drawn by him. There couldn't have been a more graphic instance of the depth of social conditioning of the human mind. Likewise, in "Initiation", the subversive potential of the act of writing occurs to Banka in an epiphanic dream sequence which takes him back to that milestone moment in his childhood when, following his ear piercing, he was initiated into the "ethos of letters" and drew with a piece of chalk three circles or zeros which stand for the Hindu trinity of Brahma, Vishnu and Maheswar, the symbols respectively of the Creator, the Preserver and the Destroyer.

## Epiphanies: Soul Freedom

Dreams are of course vitally connected with another kind of unconscious showing forth which comes to us as a flash, as an inner vision, as a moment of discovery, and which goes by the name that Joyce gave to his literary technique, namely epiphany. It is epiphanies that liberally intersperse the narrative of *Banka Harichandan*. And they don't have to come upon him as a visitation, as in dreams, but may occur quietly in the course of a matter-of-fact day, as in Joyce's *Dubliners* stories. These epiphanies feature either children or childlike adults as Banka's mentors. Since Banka's creator has talked about Banka's dream and desire for escape from the four oppressive "Houses of Stewardship", namely family, school, society, and religion, it is quite possible to imagine him as having thought of a grander plan for Banka to truly transform his consciousness.

Interestingly, it is not Art that is offered as the final House of Stewardship. The pattern with Joyce is broken here to introduce the Yogic principle of meditation and detachment. Two of the finest stories in the volume, namely "A Stint in Hell" and "Alone", show Banka receiving his early training in being weary of the world of surface appearances and senses which are the source of all delusions and illusions. Both the stories are also structured in a similar way, with an early descent into hell—gluttony in case of the first, and a possible blindness in case of the second—and a glimpse of the road less travelled at the end through a transforming journey or insight.

It is significant that Banka's mentors are very much outside of the rulebook. The first mentor is the childlike middle Mama (maternal uncle) of "A Stint in Hell" who teaches him to value manual work and to not despise menial labour, even of the scavenging kind. The second mentor is the blind boy philosopher in "Alone", Ainthu, who reminds him of the "sins" that eyes can commit.

> Do you know my grandma always said one thing when I was a child? "This Ainthu is a blessed soul. Sin will not touch him. Ninety-nine percent of our sins are committed by this accursed pair of eyes."

Banka is made sharply aware here of the "visual rape" he committed the night before.

> Banka was immediately reminded of the dirty pictures and descriptions in the books on Chacha's shelf which he had spied upon last evening.

It is the lesson of the *Gita* that quietly reverberates in the background as the blind Ainthu delivers his words of wisdom nonchalantly. Banka most closely resembles Salinger's Teddy in these epiphanic moments. He becomes Teddy, re-imagined and resurrected in the Odishan context.

The traffic of influence is, of course, never one-way, meaning from American or Western culture towards Odia or Indian or Eastern culture. As anyone who has read Salinger's "Teddy" is aware, the realisation of the failure to lead a truly moral and spiritual life in America, the bastion of consumerism, has made Teddy lean more and more towards a notion of bhakti-based spirituality, harboured in ancient Indian culture, rather than through reason, argument and analysis. Teddy's vision of the reform of the American education system with its stress on meditation and on the unity of life grasped at a supra-sensory level, rather than on sense objects and on surface forms, shows this influence of Indian thought clearly. In a sense Banka in these two stories pays back to Teddy. But Teddy is already a debtor of Indian culture. The debt is thus two-way, reciprocal.

## Conclusion

Banka is not on a higher moral ground than the children, the boys and the adolescents with whom he shares his existential space within the world of literature. This is in contrast to how Teddy is imagined, as several cuts above the American characters he circulates among. This is because of Teddy's mystical access to an alternative philosophy—read Indian—of life, while Banka, frustrated by a scheme of things too narrow and oppressive—small-towny, utilitarian, financially straitened, colonial and hierarchical—is seen struggling throughout for self-actualisation.

Banka can have a clear-eyed perception of his condition as a victim or scapegoat most of the time and can only sporadically rise towards fragmented flashes of illumination about his own swadharma, his true self or calling. It's only in the last story of the series, "On the Edge", that he has a conscious life-altering moment of clarity.

> Would Bajrangbali, his companion during all his lonely and frightful moments, be able to deliver him from this hell of aloneness? Perhaps not. But he still felt a strong wave of resolution welling up inside him. If this hell was his fate, his ultimate destiny, then he would delve deep into its bottomless pit, fully conscious. An endless fall into that hell was far better than the deceptions involved in keeping up appearances.

It becomes crystal clear to him that he must fall and fall alone and embrace both his failing and aloneness, much like Stephen in Joyce's *A Portrait of the Artist as a Young Man*, if he must write the rules of engagement anew.

It is time to draw the curtain on this rather long introduction by saying Banka Harichandan is not an extraordinary boy; he is one of us. *The Life and Times of Banka Harichandan* is an extraordinary tale of an ordinary boy, told in a touchingly light vein.[6] And in this lies its lasting value.

## Coda: A Note on Translation

"The Account of a Pilgrimage" was published to much readerly attention in 2001. As a colleague of the author at the English department of Utkal University at that point of time, I was hit by the ripple effects of the splash more than most. The desire to translate the story was spawned in me almost immediately. It was a mere flicker of a desire, as it turned out, for the translation never got off the ground. Looking back, I realise that the temptation to be a part of the newly unfolding translation activism in Odisha's academic and cultural life had something to do with the desire. Many like me jumped or wanted to jump onto the translation bandwagon. I personally failed then because I lacked the conviction that translation was a worthy enterprise as well as the skill required for moving between Odia and English. It would take close to twenty years before the interrupted translational journey would be resumed. But first, a few quick words about the status

6. It is perhaps the appropriate moment to say a word about the strange-looking title of the coming-of-age narrative of Banka Harichandan. Insofar as the light-hearted contents of the narrative are at odds with a title that echoes the solidity of the bildungsroman, it is an ironic title. But then it is also in earnest as a title, concerned with retrieving from oblivion the long lost country of childhood where sensations are at their sharpest and most pristine.

of Odia Literature in English translation as it developed in the meantime.

Since the start of the twenty-first century, globalisation quickened its inroads into Odia culture, as it did in other non-metro and less heavily industrialised societies of India, in a big way. One of its effects was a renewed investment of energy in translating into English. This was because Odisha keenly felt the need for international exposure made possible by globalisation. Interestingly, however, the translations during this period did not take the form of an "ethno-centric" practice of "Englishing", as had been the case with the minuscule, random and sporadic English language translation efforts seen in the last three decades of the twentieth century. On the contrary, spurred by globalisation's unintended consequence of local cultural reawakening, an "ethno-deviant" practice of translating took hold, a practice that could paradoxically create a place for Odia literature and culture at the global table but on its own terms, that is, by showcasing the culture's unique flavour and identity.

In the first half of the first decade of the twenty-first century, a multi-author English translation project[7]

7. It was a team of four translators that was involved in this landmark translation of *Chha Mana Atha Guntha*. They are Rabi Shankar Mishra, Jatindra K. Nayak, Satya P. Mohanty, and Paul St-Pierre. The first two are professors of English in Odisha. Mohanty is professor of English at Cornell University, USA. Paul St-Pierre is professor of Translation at Montreal University, Canada. They began work on the translation in the later part of 1990 and completed the work in 2004–05.

focused on the first modern, realistic and satirical Odia novel, *Chha Mana Atha Guntha* (1902) by Fakir Mohan Senapati (1843–1918), was the sensational news from the frontlines of the Odisha translation scene. It was a symbol of Odia cultural resurgence in a globalised world, and, fittingly enough, it took as its object as well as inspiration, a novel that embodied a similar cultural resurgence of the Odia nation, trenchantly voiced by Senapati, at the turn of the nineteenth century. The English translation entitled *Six Acres and a Third* was published by the University of California Press in 2005. It became the trigger for a huge tidal wave of translations into English that continues to this day.

This is, of course, retrospective theorising on my part, for I understood the dynamics of the new translational activism in Odisha much later in the course of my academic and critical work. Anyway, this awareness brought with it a renewed desire to translate. So, in the intervening years, and especially since 2018, I was reborn as a translator. Of course, the return to Pattanaik's story was delayed by other pressing projects that got my attention between 2019 and 2021. The delay, I thought was good, not only because I was convinced and ready to undertake the translation but also because Pattanaik had in the meantime built a sizeable and respectable body of work of short fiction, of which the corpus centred on his child protagonist Banka was unquestionably the most significant. As I have indicated earlier in this introduction, there was a book in Odia already in existence, containing eight such stories, with four new stories freshly generated. Banka Harichandan seemed poised to be reborn, and, this time through a vigorous translational mediation. *The Life and Times of Banka Harichandan* took shape in 2022 as my fifth translation project. The choice of the title, suggested by the author, was spot on. Whatever else I may have added to or subtracted from the book, I have kept faith with the name.

So how did I go about translating the original stories in Odia which aim at narrating the coming-of-age story of a hypersensitive and precocious boy, together with his perception, cognition and sensation in an "idiolect" all his own? The defining aspect of this idiolect is that it is a colloquial speech rhythm in which key information is often not stated because it is understood by members of a "high-context" (read Odia) culture. A very good example occurs in the first line of the opening story "An Inauspicious Morning in the Life of Banka Harichandan": "In the dead of the night Banka woke up with a start." The Odia original goes like this: "majhi ratire hatat nida bhangigala." The literal rendering would be: "In the middle of the night sleep was suddenly broken." The question "whose sleep?" will normally not tend to be asked of the Odia sentence as it would be of the literal English sentence if it is the opening line of a story. That is why, in my rendering the subject or the doer of the action needed to be specified through direct naming, as in the above instance, or through a controlled supply of contextual cues, as in the opening sentence of the ninth story "Rain Cycle" ("Banka was initiated into Bollywood lore through Chiku bhai, the neighbourhood gossip"). The original, as may be safely presumed, does not have the qualifier "the neighbourhood gossip".

Another aspect of Banka's idiolect concerns the use of the highly informal and indecorous home and street lingo. I will once again provide an example from the opening of the first story where Banka is thinking about his Chacha's (Uncle's) uncontrolled anger: "After failing the B.A. exam again this time Chacha was acting like a wild bull." The Odia version is this: "eithara bie fail hela pare khali arana mainsi bhali hausunti." The word "hausunti" is a colloquial word, used by illiterate and semi-literate folks. Its literal translation would be "behaving", which, in English, completely neutralises the colloquial flavour. If we use English words which go with a wild bull, such as "stomp" or "rampage", then the word exceeds its grasp if ever so slightly. Hence I have settled for an in between word, "act". It is also notable that once again the subject of the action, "Chacha" is unstated.

So, my translation strategy was underpinned by the need to transfer language in this narrative—and, of course, feelings and ideas bound up with it—from a "high-context" source culture (one where things are understood without being made explicit) to a "low context" target culture (one where such detailing and explicit naming is necessary). This would make the first version, the one featured in this translation, appear more desirable.

We can look at another example of this from the story "Timetable". In this the memory of the Mathematics teacher pressing the cheek of Banka's adolescent flame, Preeti, in mock anger, flits through Banka's mind for an instant when he is playing cricket, making his bowling go haywire. The original has this: "chhaka pare chhaka nadi deijiba Banka ta laya pheripaiba paryanta." Rendered literally, it would be "would pile sixer after sixer till Banka gets back his concentration." The same dropped subject (Kama bhai) and the same clipped and colloquial idiom here ("nadideijiba"), which would be inadequate for the reader from the "low context" culture, unless drawn out a little: "He would tear into the bowling, hitting a flurry of sixes till Banka got back his concentration."

The question then is this: does it have to be the middle style, as in the above examples? Or will the low, racy style be more suitable? Here I have made the conscious choice to opt for the middle style. This is based on two considerations. One is that the middle style would guard against the "naturalising" of the text to which racy and idiomatic English will render it liable. The world being depicted in the *Banka* narrative is one saturated with a semi-provincial Odia landscape and ethos, with English constituting a superimposed aspirational language for the middle and lower middle class. We must not lose sight of this in the translation. The second consideration—and it is an important one—is that it would be relatively easier, perched on the middle style, to take those occasional flights into a slightly decorous, elevated language that the narrator sometimes uses to convey heightened feelings that Banka's inward-bound trajectory necessarily evokes.

One example of the leap will suffice. It is from "First Separation".

Egged on by his street-loafing friends, Banka is wondering about the meaning of "masti" that laying with a woman is supposed to give. He looks up the word "masti" in a number of dictionaries that his father has on his shelf. To no avail, for "fun", its most obvious sense, does not correspond to the "masti" of "romp". Banka instinctively knows that there's a hiatus between the meaning of a word in the dictionary and "the experience to which it beckoned". And then one day, he catches sight of the young, nine or ten-year old girl living near his house. It is the sighting of her receding frock rather. The meaning of "masti", couched in the following expression, suddenly bursts upon him.

> But when Banka's eyes met hers, the girl smiled at him and ran away inside, letting go of her mother's pallu. The sight of her evanescing frock was almost like a scorpion sting that released a generous dose of venom into his blood stream. Although Mother had not opened up about this before, Banka realised that, apart from money corruptly earned, there were a thousand other things in this world, capable of making your heart race like mad, as though from a whiplash of venom.

This is only purportedly child-Banka's language. Actually, it is the language of the adult narrator for a thirteen or fourteen-year old adolescent. Not only are the Odia expressions used to describe "evanescing frock" and "venom" from a higher register ("apasruyamana", "jahara"), the entire drift of meaning in this sentence, as in the narrative as a whole, is towards a rarefied region where writing earns its keep not simply by referencing the world but by becoming finely wrought. Both the original *Banka Harichandan* and the copy, namely the translation, are agreed on this. Thus the translation exudes the flavour of the Odia story even in its non-identity and difference.

Another important strategy I have followed is to not burden the translation with a plethora of culture-specific words in transliteration, as is increasingly the practice in contemporary English-language translation from Indian languages. It was necessary, however, to retain a handful of culture-specific words (like "aarti" in "Resolution", "abhada" in "The Account of a Pilgrimage", not to mention Odia markers of exclamation such as "arrey" that the narrative is liberally spiced with) as well as some of the kinship terms such as Aai, Chacha, Nani, Bua, etc. What I did was to transliterate the term and follow it up with an immediate glossing of it in the text, which makes it clear that it is the translator's insertion. There is also the literal translation strategy that I have used to convey the flavour of the original Odia expression. Examples of this include expressions like "digging rivers of blood in the back" ("An Inauspicious Morning...") and "the water has risen to such heights" ("First Separation") etc. On the whole, my attempt has been to present *The Life and Times of Banka Harichandan* in English with just a dash of the foreign in it, which inevitably gestures towards its Odia substratum.

# AN INAUSPICIOUS MORNING IN THE LIFE OF BANKA HARICHANDAN

*Translated from "Banka Harichandan Jibanare Eka Ashubha Sakala"*

In the dead of the night, Banka woke with a start. What time could it be? Three o'clock? His throat was parched. Banka lay close to the wall. Chacha—Father's younger brother—was at the other end of the bed. Banka's elder sister and younger brother slept in-between. To get down from the cot one had to cross them all. Grandmother lay on a mat on the floor beside the cot. If you stepped on her, you'd be done for. God knows when she would have caught some sleep, huffing and puffing in asthma through the long night. She would curse for a long time if her sleep was disturbed. If Chacha was woken up by her shout then it would be all over for you: he would beat you to a pulp.

After failing the B.A. exam again this time Chacha was acting like a wild buffalo. He had failed twice before. Last time when Father heard he had flunked, he had slapped Chacha so hard that he had collapsed on the floor like a felled tree. Then Father said, "You fail again, and it will be good-bye to your studies. Take a loan and drive an auto-rickshaw." Hearing this, Sipra, the next-door neighbour's daughter, was so tickled that she left the place stifling her laughter with the end of her saree. But Banka and company were trembling to their bones at the scene they had just witnessed. If adults could be thrashed like this, Banka thought to himself, what would be the fate of children like him? He prayed hard to Lord Mahadeva, the presiding deity of the local cremation ground, and hoped that he would be spared the ordeal of appearing at the B.A. exams.

His fear of Grandma's curse and Chacha's anger could have stifled his thirst but Banka felt a strong urge to pee as well. On one hand the urge to relieve the growing pressure in the bladder, and, on the other hand, the craving to drink some water. Caught between the two, he cursed the summer season till his heart was content and decided to risk climbing down from the cot. He crawled across his elder sister first and then Chhotu, his younger brother. After he crossed the first obstacle he stretched one leg straight towards the floor. Once he felt his foot touch the ground he swung his other leg over Chacha and stood on the floor. Fortunately, Grandma was lying some distance away from the cot. He had no difficulty tip-toeing over her. Then he remembered it is not auspicious to tip-toe over a sleeping person in that manner. When Chhotu was just a kid he had jumped over him playfully and Mother had asked him not to do that. If you jump over somebody like that his life-span gets shortened. But he realised he had no qualms about jumping over grandma. He thought to himself, her life-span should be shortened, the bloody old woman. She should die as soon as possible. It would serve her right. Cursing through the day and nursing asthma through the night. Not even serving a proper meal to them after Father and Mother went to Bombay. She is feeding the Chachas well. If Banka happens to be around while San Chacha is eating, she starts swearing and cursing "these god-forsaken gluttons". She rations his meals under the plea that he might fall ill due to overeating, because of which Banka feels pangs of hunger throughout the school hours. Banka thought to himself he should jump over Grandma ten to twenty times while she is asleep so that her life-span would be shortened drastically. But as soon as this thought crossed his mind he felt guilty. This kind of thinking is not good. If you think ill of somebody it rebounds on you, Mother had said. For this evil thought he prayed to Lord Hanuman and asked for forgiveness. To ward off any possible harm to himself, he recited the Hanuman Chalisa silently.

Reciting still, he slowly unlocked and opened the door to the backyard. The yard was bright with moonlight. But the lingering darkness might still contain a few ghosts and evil spirits. He quickened the recitation of the Hanuman Chalisa and from the edge of the veranda itself started peeing with full force onto the yard underneath. He felt a pang of fear as soon as he finished. Could the sound have wakened Chacha? Thank God, no one had been disturbed. He closed the door silently. Picked up a torch from Mother's dressing table and shuffled across to the pitcher of water in the kitchen. He poured some water into the mug that covered the mouth of the pitcher and started sipping the water noisily. At the first contact of water with his dry throat his thirst burst forth like the holy fire that jumps up from the pit of a yajna when ghee is poured on it. After a few moments he felt comforted. In the torchlight the table clock read 4:30, not 3 o'clock, as he had thought earlier. At that very moment, as if to confirm the time by the clock, the terrible shriek of a bird sounded from somewhere. That was followed by the twitter of several birds as the sky became brighter. After replacing the torch Banka went back to his assigned corner on the cot carefully. He lay there, eyes closed, but sleep eluded him. The guilt for the evil thought he had nursed against Grandma kept goading him. He tried to console his own mind, but to no avail. I wished her death for her own good, he reasoned to himself. Has she not been suffering badly due to her asthma? Death would be deliverance for her really. Her own welfare drove me to think like that, not my malice for her. Does Mother not wish to die when he is naughty? That is just a playful death-wish. One really doesn't have to die if somebody was slightly naughty! That is the kind of playful death-wish he had for Grandma. Not real, he went on consoling his mind which wouldn't be comforted.

The twittering of birds became more intense as time

went by. As if there was a contest going on among the birds to outshout each other. Banka turned his attention towards the sound. Engrossed, he almost lost track of time. The variety of bird-song overwhelmed him. This must be a blue jay, this a crow, this a myna, this a golden oriole. Guests visit your house if you sight a golden oriole. Should he go out and track a golden oriole? God knows how long Father and Mother have been gone from home. There was no sign of their return. The hospital is somewhere in a far-off city. That is the only place where Mother's disease could be treated. The city Bombay, how long does it take to get there by train? Banka was confused. The golden oriole might have vanished in the meantime. But he was happy for the fact that he was able to recognise the birds from their twitter. He had heard bird-song before, but not with so much attention this early in the morning. A gust of wind blew the window screen. From the bed Banka had a brief glimpse of the yard outside when the screen swung open. What did he see? A single myna on the branch of the guava tree. His heart skipped a beat. To sight a single myna is not a good omen at all. Now he could easily overcome his fear of Chacha and Grandma and rushed out of bed towards the window. He shuffled the window screen fully open and had a good look across the yard. There was not a single soul out there. He thought if he could locate a myna couple, at least he could escape his inauspicious fate for the day. But where is the other myna? The single myna was still perched on the branch with a gloomy mien. Now... now, this single myna too flew away even as Banka was desperately searching for its partner among the branches. His chest started thumping like a threshing-horse. Something terrible is in the offing today. Now he remembered he had stolen a look at the sky while pissing. There was a single star in the sky. 'One star kills men, two stars...' while playing the game of bride-theft Puni used to sing this rhyme she had learnt from her grandma. Apprehension of some unknown fear made his body sweat, although the fan was at its full speed. He was now convinced that because of the evil thought he had nursed against his grandma he was facing so many bad omens this early in the morning.

Presently Grandma woke up. For some reason Banka felt a great surge of affection for her. He sidled up to her and lay by her side, seeking a snuggle. "Hey, leave me alone. Aren't you too old for this tomfoolery?" Grandma croaked, her voice choked with early morning gruffness. Still, somehow he relished the sweetness of her reprimand. At least, the reprimand was less painful than the fear he was feeling inside. Maybe her reprimand would absolve him of the guilt he felt from wishing for her early death a little while ago.

Grandma stepped out of the room and opened the door to the courtyard. Now it was brighter. The sound of the bird-twitter was increasingly stifled under the din of the town, the ringing bells of cycle rickshaws, the sound of water flowing from taps in the houses of the neighbours. The wind of the electric fan mixed with the early morning air outside was probably too cool for Chacha, so he wrapped himself with the bed-sheet he was sleeping on and went for his second round of sleep. Nani, his elder sister, was not up yet. She was usually the first to leave the bed. She puts paste on his toothbrush. She opens Chhotu's mouth and cleans his teeth for him. Today, Banka is free to do as he pleases. He pumped a large quantity of paste out of the tube onto his toothbrush. Nani rations out a small quantity of paste every day. Now that he had as much as he wanted he quickly put it in his mouth along with the toothbrush and went out into the front-yard facing the street. The taste of paste was sweet and cool initially, but then it quickly changed into a painful sensation of burning. He quickly spat out few gobs of rapidly forming spittle and felt some relief. But by that time the foam of the paste and saliva from the mouth had wetted his palm. The moment Banka brought the brush out of his mouth to check how much paste was still smeared on the brush it slipped out of his palm and fell straight into the municipality drain beside the street.

Banka felt as if somebody had struck a heavy blow to his chest. His entire body shook in fright. He was now convinced that the inauspicious day had already started unfolding. Otherwise why did he come to the front yard instead of the backyard, as was his wont, to finish brushing his teeth? Why did he smear such a large quantity of toothpaste on his brush? If Chacha came to know his merciless thrashing would dig rivers of blood on his back. He might manage to hide the fact for a day or two. But at some point Chacha would come to know about the missing toothbrush. How long could he hide the fact of the missing toothbrush?

Instead of wasting time on fruitless thought, Banka went down the steps towards the drain. The putrid waste-material had turned the water black. The brush had sunk somewhere without a trace. The water was stagnant and had a foul smell. He knew neighbourhood urchins defecated in the drain but despite his revulsion he stirred the drain with a branch he broke from a nearby bush. There was no trace of the green-coloured toothbrush anywhere but the vigorous stirring of the drain filled the air with such a stench that he felt like vomiting. Luckily, he had not had his breakfast otherwise he would surely have vomited. When he realised the pointlessness of his efforts after two to three minutes of stirring the drain with a branch, he held his breath, closed his eyes and shoved his left arm into the sticky, decomposed, foul smelling waste material in the drain. He remembered the story from the Mahabharat his mother had told him about how for telling a single lie the virtuous Yudhishthira had to dip his little finger in hell. He had committed a more heinous sin by wishing for Grandma's early death. He felt as if God had meted out instant punishment for his sin. But a far graver crisis was that the toothbrush could not be traced. If he failed to recover the toothbrush Chacha's blows and slaps would be more unbearable than God's punishment in hell. Banka vigorously scooped out fistfuls of decomposed waste material from the drain without bothering about the dirt and stench. God knows how long he would have ploughed the drain for his brush, but Chhotu suddenly showed up and asked, "What are you up to, brother?"

Banka had not realised when Chhotu had come to the front veranda and had discovered him near the drain. Banka hastily got up and blurted out, "Chhotu, want to eat a chocolate? A big chocolate?" Chhotu nodded his head in assent.

"Don't tell Chacha my eraser fell here in the drain." Banka tried to placate.

"But you are lying. You don't have any money, how will you buy chocolate for me?"

Banka had not really thought about the money angle. When Mother was around one could steal a rupee or fifty paise tied to the end of her saree. Now even she was not around.

"My friend Harish has promised to share some chocolates with me. His Chacha has brought them from foreign". Banka blurted out a lie. And then he hurried towards the bathroom lest Chhotu should ask some more uncomfortable questions. In the bathroom he took a cake of soap and washed his left arm with it diligently. Then he remembered Harish. No, not for the chocolate he had promised Chhotu. He could buy a new toothbrush by borrowing some money from Harish. For the first time that morning he felt a sense of relief after he hit upon this plan.

Harish lived at the end of their street. His father was a

policeman probably. He wore a khaki dress occasionally. Every day they cooked fish or chicken for dinner. Harish's mother gave him five to ten rupees as pocket money to spend. He also stole money from his father's pocket once in a while. If he was in the mood, he treated Banka and his other friends to ice-cream. Banka's father was a big officer too, but he never received that kind of pocket money. Harish became his classmate after failing twice in the annual exam. Banka topped in the class regularly, but he felt small in the presence of Harish because the latter had money. He suffered all of Harish's lewd pranks and banter in silence. Once he wrote an obscene letter and asked Banka to place it inside Kuni's notebook surreptitiously, of course, in exchange for a bribe of fifteen rupees. But Banka flatly denied the offer. Harish swore that he loved Kuni. In the fitness of things he should put the letter, Banka retorted. Harish then explained to him that no one would suspect Banka because he was a good student. Now Banka decided to accept Harish's offer of placing his letter in Kuni's notebook in exchange for fifteen rupees with which he could buy a new toothbrush and escape Chacha's thrashing. When Mother comes back he would return Harish's money and end this evil relationship.

After washing his hand, Banka saw that Chacha was still asleep. Nani was helping Chhotu brush his teeth. Now was the right time. He slowly slunk away from home and started walking towards Harish's house. He crossed the quarters of the Lady Doctor on his way. Her husband was in the garden tending the flower bed, with his back to the street. He quickly went past the yard in order to avoid getting noticed by him. Harish had warned him earlier "Never go near the old man. He will give it to you where it hurts most."

Banka did not understand what Harish meant. The man was a good-for-nothing, always liked children and shared guavas from his garden. Much later Banka found out why Harish had asked him not to go anywhere near the old man. Once in the evening Chacha had sent him to fetch some paan for him. Chacha was not good at studies but was a real music aficionado. When Father and other elder Chachas were not around, harmonium in hand, he would set up his music party on the roof-top. Friends would turn up. Sharbat would be served. Paan laced with lime and tobacco would be ordered. On those occasions Banka would be called upon to fetch paan.

One of those evenings the squint-eyed Chheta was sitting beside the paan-shop. He was the local goon who looked like the very devil with one normal eye and the other white like a ping-pong ball. This white eye-ball made his visage hideous. The squint-eyed Chheta sold cinema tickets in the black market, drank booze, and had been to jail a few times. When he saw Banka that evening, God knows what came to his mind; he bought a huge piece of chocolate for Banka and offered it to him. Banka was hesitant.

Chheta persuaded him, "Eat, eat, don't be shy. Are you good at studies? What brings you here? Has your Chacha sent you to fetch paan?"

Banka was silent throughout Chheta's chatter. "Hey, Haria!" Chheta called out to the shopkeeper "Prepare the paan for that lecher. Once you are through give us a shout. We are waiting."

After saying this, Chheta held his wrist and literally dragged him towards the darkened space behind the shop. The place was lonely and fairly dark. Banka was terrified but was unable to extricate his hand from Chheta's grip. With a great show of affection Chheta was softly massaging his body. He also planted a couple of kisses on his cheeks. The stench of tobacco from his mouth made Banka feel like vomiting. As they sat down on a nearby culvert Chheta asked him about Sabi. When Banka struggled to extricate himself he forcibly lifted him on to his lap. Then Banka remembered the warning Harish gave him about the husband of the lady-doctor. With one brutal thrust Banka freed himself from his clutches and swiftly ran home. When Chacha asked him about the paan, he said that he lost the money somewhere. Chacha gave him a tight slap across his cheek. But for the first time in his life he didn't mind being beaten up by Chacha.

Deep in thoughts about Chheta and the husband of the lady-doctor, Banka realised that he had crossed the temple of goddess Mangala and was almost near Harish's house. Seeing him from the rooftop, Harish came out of the house to the street. "Hello Mr. Bankanidhi, where to?" Harish greeted him. He was the only person who called him by his full name. Banka had a cleft on his lower lip from birth, so people called him Banka, the curved one. Later, he was also given the name of Bankanidhi.

"Do you know they have come back? I saw Sabi near the water-front when I went with father to fetch fresh fish." Banka was terrified as he heard him. He completely forgot about the deal of love-letter and fifteen rupees as he started perspiring profusely. How happy he had been when they had run away from the town! He had offered two bananas in the temple of goddess Mangala. It was hardly two months and now they were back. An unknown fear gripped him.

"I am going back. If Chacha wakes up, he will be mad. I have not done my homework yet."

"Did you come to visit the temple?"

"Yes" Banka lied.

"Let us go to the market square. We can have some tea and smoke bidis." Harish suggested.

Once or twice he had smoked bidis with Harish and his nostrils had been in flames for a long time. Now already he was under great stress after hearing about Chheta and Sabi's return. He did not agree with Harish's suggestion.

"I have not finished my arithmetic lesson. Let us smoke on our way to school." Banka said as he hurried back.

At home he found Nani and Chhotu at breakfast, munching on last night's left-over chapatis along with raw cooking oil, salt and onions. Nani was also nibbling on a green chilli between helpings of chapati and onion.

Between mouthfuls of food Nani admonished him, "Where are you roaming around, you scoundrel! Let Chacha get up, I will tell him."

On a different day Banka would have given her a fitting retort. But he realised it was an inauspicious day today; one accident had followed another from the moment he left his bed, and kept quiet. Hurriedly he poured two buckets of water on himself and sat down for breakfast. Nani handed him his share of chapati. In the kitchen Grandma was boiling something, as the whistle of the pressure-cooker indicated. Probably she was preparing breakfast for Chacha. Chacha never ate last night's food. Every morning Grandma prepared fresh upma, halwa or something fried for him. After Chacha had his fill, Grandma would share the remainder with them.

Banka had no appetite today, although he munched on the stale chapati in a desultory manner. A nameless fear had killed all his appetite. He quickly swallowed the food and washed it down with a glass of water. Before Nani could instruct him, he opened his school bag and sat down to solve arithmetic sums. But the letters and numbers on the book appeared blurry to his eyes. His mind was in a whirl after Harish had informed him about the return of Chheta and Sabi. He remembered the day Sabi had eloped. Sabi's mother had been howling inconsolably.

His own mother had checked her box of ornaments, money-purse and the almirah to verify whether Sabi had stolen anything. Amidst all this, however, Banka was very happy. He had offered two bananas to goddess Mangala that day. Not that he disliked Sabi. In fact she liked him a lot. But three to four days before she eloped with the squint-eyed Chheta, he had been horrified at the way she'd behaved with him. He had gone to Puni's house to invite her to play with them. Her grandmother was feeding her at that time. The old woman was cross when Banka beckoned her:

"What kind of game will a young woman play with the boys?"

As Banka was making an about turn on hearing this, the old woman added, "These beggarly children are turning up precisely at meal-times."

His mother overheard her last statement. My God, one could only imagine her fiery avatar after that. Picking up a piece of fire-wood she started beating him right in Puni's courtyard so brutally that his entire body was covered in large welts. Fortunately, Sabi was getting ready to clean the plates and utensils. She immediately dropped the utensils and enfolded him, getting hit once or twice by Mother's fire-wood. But she fully sheltered him under her embrace and took him to a safe place in the backyard. All the while she was heaping the filthiest abuses upon Puni's grandmother.

Banka was sobbing inconsolably on Sabi's bosom. Sabi escorted him to a spot underneath the huge jack-fruit tree in the backyard. She kept him pressed over her bosom even after he stopped sobbing. When he was younger he used to sleep like this on his mother's bosom. Now after Chhotu's birth Mother did not allow him this luxury. The smell of her body was different. He felt breathless under her tight grip. When he tried to wriggle out of her embrace, she tightened her grip further and rolled down on the ground with him. She held him between her thighs and forced his hand to touch her. Banka was in real panic. Harish had told him earlier that if a boy and a girl become one like this, then a child was born. Banka used all his strength and kicked her away. Then he ran back to the house. Sabi was not offended. Rather she mocked him from behind, "You just wait for me, Banka. Let me tell your mother what you were up to in the backyard."

Sabi did not carry out her threat. As usual she cleaned the utensils and finished her other chores. Banka kept a strict eye on her. One day passed. Two days went by. Days rolled on, but Sabi did not tell on him. Banka was assured that Sabi would not complain to his mother after all. But if she gave birth to a child then everyone would come to know automatically. He continued to remain besieged by fear. Then one day, to his great relief, she eloped with the squint-eyed Chheta. People said that they had run away from the town. Some others claimed that Chheta had given ten thousand rupees to her alcoholic father in exchange for Sabi. Her mother's ranting was only for show. But after that incident Banka was in great peace of mind.

He was again gripped by fear when Harish informed

him that they were back in town. What a horrible beginning to the morning! First the evil thoughts about Grandmother, then the sighting of a lone myna followed by a single star in the sky, and then losing the toothbrush in the drain... What other dangers lurked for him that day? Who knows? His entire body started shaking with some unknown fear. He tried to divert his mind towards theorems of geometry. He could not remember a word. He tried to work out some arithmetic sums on the floor with a chalk in hand. The usual problems of arithmetic like the ascent of a monkey on a slippery pole, the water-tank fed by two taps with varying speeds which he could usually solve easily with his left-hand, so to say, defied him. He left arithmetic and tried to study English grammar, then from grammar he shifted to literature, and from there to social science. He ran his eyes over all kinds of textbooks but he could not dispel the feeling of fear and restlessness. After some thought he decided to inform Chacha about Chheta and Sabi's return to town, although he was convinced that any exchange would be but an invitation to a sound thrashing from Chacha.

Still, with great trepidation he tip-toed towards the kitchen. Grandma was making potato fritters. Chacha was gorging upon them, his back towards Banka. When Grandmother saw him approaching, she mocked at him, "We know why you are shuffling around the place in this manner." She was obviously hinting at Banka's gluttony, but eating fritters was far from his mind at that time, so he ignored Grandmother's banter.

Chacha turned around and shouted, "Where have you been roaming this morning, you scoundrel, leaving your studies?"

Banka's innards were contorted due to fear. With great difficulty he stopped his tears from bursting forth and said, "Chacha, they have come back."

Chacha raised his voice further and shouted, "Who? Who has come back? You invent all kinds of alibis to avoid studying, it seems."

Grandma was moved by Banka's pitiable condition. She admonished Chacha, "Don't shout, the child might be missing his parents." Then she asked him, "Do you miss your father and mother? Who has come back?"

Banka wanted to say that Chheta, the goon, and Sabi, the maid, had come back. But his mouth was full of spittle and his chest was choked with sobs. His throat was terribly sore from the effort of stifling his sobbing. He could no more control himself after he heard the kind words from Grandmother. He burst into a flood of tears and could only manage to nod his head. Whether it was due to his inability to come out with what he wanted to say or because he was reminded of his parents, he went on sobbing piteously even as he tried to wipe off his tears with the back of his hands.

# A STINT IN HELL

*Translated from "Narka Bhoga"*

With a deafening gum gum the train came charging down with such speed that Banka thought it would simply rush past them without stopping. The sudden hooting of a horn at that very moment startled him, making him grab Mother's hand tightly. Sadly, Father noticed this and said, "This fellow is a coward, and I was thinking that I would get him admitted in the military."

It was as if a large blob of spittle had been voided upon the excitement of going to Aai's—his maternal grandmother's—village. Banka's mind was clouded over with anger and anguish. Presently the black engine and a bunch of compartments started to advance beyond where they were standing on the platform. In order to show he had not panicked at the sound of the horn he asked, "Father, won't this train stop?"

It was unclear whether his father heard his question amidst the cacophonous din of the platform, but within moments the gigantic vehicle came to a halt, panting and puffing. The coolie, carrying their belongings on his head, walked towards a certain compartment. Holding a bag in one hand and Nani's hand in another, Father followed him. Carrying Chhotu in her arms, Mother led Banka along after them. After they boarded the compartment, Father paid the coolie and set to arranging their belongings on the overhead racks. As directed by him, Mother and Nani occupied two window seats. Banka was asked to sit near Mother and Chhotu. Seating himself down near Nani, Father instructed him, "Keep an eye on the belongings."

Banka had a desire to sit by the window to watch the fast-moving scenes on the way. But it would be asking for trouble if he nagged about that. If a fist or two landed on his back in front of strangers, he would not be able to raise his face for shame throughout the journey. He cursed Nani silently and sat quietly with his eyes fixed on the belongings. Only in order to please Father.

After some time when the train began its journey two men with thick moustaches came and sat down near him. Only then Banka realised why Father had asked Mother and Nani to take the window seat. Buoyed up by a spirit of manliness, he silently congratulated Father and vowed to himself, "When I grow up I will definitely join the military and protect the country from enemies." His enthusiasm doubled, Banka sat with his back erect.

"In what class are you studying?" One of the moustachioed men suddenly asked him.

"Class five," he answered without shifting his attention from the belongings.

"Have you appeared at the scholarship examination?"

"Yes," Banka answered again with a straight face. He felt a surge of courage while saying this. He remembered the story of Casabianca. The brave young boy was burnt to death with the flaming ship just because he had given word to his father not to leave the post assigned to him. While answering the questions too, Banka's eyes did not stray from their belongings. He suspected that the men must be thieves. Why would they ask so many questions otherwise? He was feeling sleepy because he had woken up too early in the morning. But he sat, wide awake and alert, because of the moustachioed man's questions. Casabianca had not been afraid of death. Wouldn't Banka be able to perform this minor task assigned to him by his father? Couldn't he keep an alert eye on their belongings for the entire length of the train journey? If not, how would he join the military?

Even while he kept watch over their belongings he could see from the corner of his eye swiftly passing crests of temples, their walls, ponds, women bathing in those ponds, the barren fields, stray cows and goats grazing in those fields, the parrot tree and gulmohar trees whose bright red flowers had covered their branches and leaves, and once in a while, golden shower trees with their yellow flowers. Ah! Had he sat near the window he could have seen many more things. Later, he could have narrated the scenery in his essay-writing class. Nanda Sir would have been happy reading those essays. But alas, the fast-moving scenery was vanishing after getting caught in the corner of the eyes only for a moment. He was peeved with Nani. Look, how she was sitting all decked up, her hair braided and tied into a flower knot with a new ribbon. She had her eyes almost sandwiched between the railings of the window, as if she was soaking everything in. Father was preoccupied too. After instructing him to keep an eye on the belongings he became immersed in the newspaper *Prajatantra*. Mother was giving some water to a fidgety Chhotu. He tried to console himself "Okay, let Nani watch if she is so keen. She can never join the military. When I become a military officer shall I not see many things? Nani, Mother, Father, even Chhotu, cannot become military." He felt pity for them.

As a certain station approached the train halted after a lot of gasping. Banka became more alert while some passengers got off and a few others came on board the compartment. The man with the moustache lit a cigarette as the train started moving again. Banka thought Father was reading the newspaper with a great deal of attention, but the moment the cigarette was lit, he spoke in a low yet firm voice, "Please go and smoke near the door. We have children here.

The man headed quietly towards the door hearing the firmness of Father's voice. Otherwise, God only knows what Father's short-temper could have unleashed. Mother had already become anxious and was eyeing Father with concern after settling Chhotu down on the seat. The other man with the moustache, in order probably to lighten the atmosphere, looked at Father and said, "Sir, do you know one thing? This boy will earn a name when he grows up. He will be a great man." Folding the newspaper, Father only smiled a little.

"This boy has appeared at the scholarship examination, it seems. He will definitely get a scholarship."

"Let's see," Father said.

Banka was thrilled. He was expecting the discussion about his becoming a great man to continue. But Father's tone was so detached that the man did not proceed any further. Father was always like that. He was never bothered about the children's education. He might not be aware that Banka appeared at the scholarship examination, that he went to the examination centre day after day with his home tutor. After the examination, however, everyone at home said that he should have done better. How did then this person know that he would win a scholarship when his own people and his tutor were not satisfied with his performance? He must be up to some trick. Banka watched over their belongings more vigilantly.

Caught in the web of those conflicting thoughts, Banka was not mindful of the distance they had covered. The elation of boarding a train for the first time had worn itself off in the meantime. Several pleasant dreams had spun themselves around the upcoming train ride much before their journey began. He had told his friends, "My youngest uncle's marriage. We will go to Grandmother's village by train. Grandmother has a huge house, garden, farming fields, mango and plantain groves. Not tiny and cramped like the houses in town."

Now the thrill of the train was gone. The same repeated thumping sounds, the intermittent noise of long whistles, trees zipping past, fields, herds of cows and goats, temples, ponds, human beings, station after station, in each station the departing crowd of strange human beings, the vendors of tea, puffed rice with masala, fried groundnuts and other sundry items, young children with runny noses and in dirty, torn pants, cleaning the floor of the compartment with their small brooms between intervals and a few beggars, hurdy-gurdy in hand, singing songs out of tune. Banka was eager to reach Aai's place as quickly as possible. Fortunately, the two moustachioed men got down at the next station, which made Banka a bit more comfortable. "Thank God, the two thieves have not stolen anything," he assured himself. Then he asked, "Father, how far?"

"Next station," said Father and started to bring down their belongings from the overhead racks.

They had come to Aai's house long ago, boarding a rickety bus. He only had a faint memory of the previous stay; the huge house, the lovely courtyard, small fish cooked in tamarind gravy, the leftover cream in the earthenware pot of milk scraped by a piece of coconut-shell, basketfuls of ripe mangoes, raw mangoes dumped in a corner on a bed of sand to ripen. Banka's mouth watered. Although he had had a heavy breakfast of mashed gram, he started feeling hungry. He felt like snacking on something from the vendors in the compartment. But it was difficult to read Father's mood. Moreover, the heat and sweat would not allow for pleasant snacking. The increasingly humid air was unable to dry up the body sweat. Banka decided not to broach the subject of snacking. They were nearing their destination. A grand feast must be waiting for them at Grandma's place. After a bath in cold water drawn from the well the meal would be all the more enjoyable. And after the meal the congregation upon a date-palm mat on the floor of the granary! Mother had told them how as young girls they spent their days playing cards through the entire afternoon inside the relatively cool atmosphere of the mud-roofed granary. Meanwhile, Banka had learnt the card-game of "Natice" by watching others play. Their neighbour's family in town played this six-player game regularly. Banka often lingered there to watch but he was never asked to join in. And at home even the idea of a card-game was a distant dream.

At Aai's place he would have his cousins, the sons and daughters of his uncles. The card-game in the cool granary would be a real treat. With this in mind he had surreptitiously tucked a pack of cards he had borrowed from Biju bhai into an obscure corner of Mother's handbag. If needed, a new pack of cards could be bought in the village market with money got from Mausa, his eldest auntie's husband. Mausa was a big officer. Whenever he would visit Banka's house, he would come in his office jeep, accompanied by his driver and peon who addressed him as "Sir". He would give everyone ten rupees. In the presence of Mausa, Mother would ask Banka not to accept the money, but after he left she would take the money away from Banka, saying "Boys would become wayward if money fell into their hands." One could buy a whole new pack of plastic cards with one rupee only. Oh, God, when will the train stop at Aai's village station?

It seemed as if God heard Banka's prayer, because the train started to slow down after blowing three long horns. Banka got up from his seat. Father shot back immediately, "Sit down, this is not the station. Someone has pulled the chain." Getting up, Father went near the door and craned his neck towards the engine. Some people were getting off the train and hurrying across the tracks. After a few moments, Father came back and spoke to no one in particular, "Bloody thieves, they board the train ticketless. What to say of these people when the Prime Minister is looting money. They have reduced the country to an empty shell."

Banka understood his father's words a little later when they strode across the platform after getting down from the train at the next station. A man was stationed near the exit. Despite the terrible summer heat he had on a pair of white trousers and a black coat. He was checking tickets. Even as Father produced their tickets from his pocket the youngest uncle gathered their belongings from the coolie who was carrying them. Following Nani, Banka hurriedly bowed down to Mama but he had already turned his back by that time.

"Hey, Budha," Mother called out to Mama. "Banka is paying his respects. He is such a fool to bow when you can't see him."

"It is alright. He bowed from behind. Thank God, he did not deliver a kick." Uncle roared in laughter as he kept their belongings in his jeep.

"The way you talk," Mother complained in mock anger, "You're soon to be married, but have not given up childish banter."

Uncle paid his respects to Father and Mother. A faint smile flashed across Father's lips briefly. Mother said, "It is okay for now, but don't talk this way with your newly-married wife."

"No, no, he will come to you for a two-month training on how to talk," Father said.

The jeep carried them towards the house. It was a long journey, almost eight kilometres from the railway station and Banka felt hungry. His mind kept wavering from the conversation going on among the adults. The road, the fields beside it, the hills appeared somewhat half-familiar. "Hello, Banka, you have appeared at the scholarship examination, I heard. How have you done?" Uncle asked at some point.

"Good," said Banka.

"What good? He never studies. What will one do with intelligence alone? He is not applying his mind at all. If he reads for fifteen minutes at a stretch, it is a great achievement for him. He will read a story book with interest, but books in his syllabus, never," Mother complained as always.

"He is just a kid. He has already studied enough for his age. He will study more as he grows up. He will study a lot," Uncle assured.

By the time the jeep reached the house, the entire village had already assembled there. Ladies started whining, holding Mother in their arms. Half-naked urchins had surrounded the jeep. Some held puffed rice in their palms; a few others were holding smaller children with runny noses on their waists. They were gaping at Banka as if they were seeing a circus joker, and also patting the jeep lovingly. Banka hurried into the house.

In the huge living room in front of the house, all the adults were sitting on a huge mat. Following Mother's earlier instruction he went around bowing to everyone one after another. Aai, her head covered with her pallu, was sitting at the farthest corner. When Banka bowed down before her she hugged him and asked, "Arrey, Banka, you plucked Kalara Kashi, I heard."

Everyone laughed. Grandma was pronouncing the word scholarship in a manner which sounded like the name of baby bitter gourd in Odia. Aja corrected her, "Not Kalara Kashi, scholar-ship."

"Oh yes, yes. That. That word is not coming into my cursed mouth," said Aai. Giving him one more hug, she moved away towards the kitchen. In one corner of the large kitchen his elder cousins, Anu bhai and Nanu bhai, were having their meal. Their mother, Banka's eldest auntie, was serving them their food. When Banka paid her his obeisance, Aai announced loudly, "Kalara-Kashi Babu has come."

Auntie said, "Okay, that is alright. You are a good student, I hear. Have you grown so thin because of your studies? Or is your father not feeding you well?'

Then she turned her attention to Nanu bhai and Anu bhai and said, “See, such a small boy, and how good he is at his studies. You two are slackers.”

A little later, raising her voice, she spoke loud enough for everyone to hear, “How will they study? Their attention is always on good food. They will not sit down to their meals if there is no fish, meat and eggs. Who will supply them with sumptuous meals regularly?”

One of the cooks joined in, “Why, their father’s income is not small. As the saying goes, those who are well-fed hanker after more.”

Auntie seemed satisfied. Banka was eyeing the fish curry with tamarind gravy on his cousins’ plates. At last, shedding his inhibitions, Banka whispered, “Aai, I am hungry.”

Grandma sent him with a domestic servant to the well. By the time Banka returned from his bath, Auntie and his cousins had vanished from the spot. There was no trace of Nani and Mother, who had melted into the group of village women.

Aai served him rice on a leaf-plate. “Shall I call Nani?” Banka suggested. “You eat first. I will take care of that spoilt girl later.”

After a couple of helpings of rice, Banka said in a low voice, “Aai, tamarind fish?”

“There is no more of it, my dear. Those two rascals have polished off all the fish curry. I will cook tamarind fish for you tomorrow,” she assured him.

But Banka’s hunger died the moment he heard her

words. Somehow he managed to put a few helpings of rice and curry into his mouth, gulped them down along with the rising frustration and drank a glass of water.

The first thing he did after the meal was to try and locate Nani. Once he saw her, he complained, "Nani, Anu bhai and Nanu bhai have finished off the tamarind fish."

Nani frowned, "Shut up."

Nobody knew where he was at that time, but Anu bhai charged towards him when he heard the exchange, "What is he saying, what is he saying, the rascal?"

Banka was scared when he saw an enraged Anu bhai. Pushing him back with one hand, he again interrogated, "Why did you come in our jeep?"

Nani answered for him in a stern manner, raising her voice, "Why are you asking him, Anu? Why don't you ask Auntie? Shall I call your father here? To settle the issue?"

Nani's raised voice drew out Manu Apa, the eldest sister of Anu bhai. When she heard what the matter was, she dragged Anu bhai away to the bedroom, holding him by the ear. Manu Apa was the eldest among all the cousins. She was in college. All the children held her in awe and reverence. She put Anu bhai on the bed and issued her firm warning, "Sleep here quietly. If you move an inch from here before four o'clock in the afternoon, then you will get it from me."

In a slightly less angry tone she commanded Banka, "You go to bed in the next room, or else I will not spare you too."

"Manu Apa, I will sleep in the granary," Banka protested faintly.

"Arrey, there are huge cobras in there. How can you even think of sleeping in the granary? Go to bed quietly. When you wake up at four, you can go there with me."

Banka was scared when he heard about the cobras, and without further ado he climbed into the bed. Grandma's cot was huge with high legs. Wooden bars with finely carved figures surrounded the bed like a fence. There was a narrow passage for one person to slip into the bed. When he climbed up onto the bed he felt like he was swimming in the sky. Sleep eluded him; thoughts about tamarind fish, Anu bhai's rudeness, Auntie's banter, the cool comfort of the granary, cobras, and the card-game "Natice" whirled in his mind. But one thing that comforted him somewhat was Nani's standing up to Anu bhai. At home, Nani always scolded him, spoke ill of him in front of Chacha, did not allow him near her when she played with her friends. For this reason, he sometimes prayed to Hanuman, "O Bajrangbali, please kill Nani. If not, make her fall ill. Make her disabled so that she will remain confined to her bed."

But the way she stood up to Anu bhai on his behalf made him feel guilty about his past behaviour. He invoked Lord Hanuman again. "O Bajrangbali, heap all good fortunes on Nani. Forget all my earlier prayers."

Banka did not realise when sleep had overtaken him while he was engaged in fervent prayers. It was evening by the time he woke up. There was deep silence all around. In a nearby cot Chhotu was sound asleep. He had been fenced around with a couple of pillows. Banka thought that Nani and his cousins were in the granary. He climbed down from the tall cot, washed his face and hurried towards the granary. The granary was at the very end after one crossed the courtyard, the store, the kitchen and the cowshed. As Banka went beyond the courtyard he noticed Anu bhai and Nanu bhai emerging from the store, their mouths stuffed with God-knows-what and huge rasgullahs in their hands. Their mother too emerged from the store after them and immediately put a big lock on the door. When they saw Banka they ran away in the opposite direction, towards the large garden surrounding the house. Banka felt a craving for rasgullah when he saw them gulping the sweetmeat, but Auntie did not notice him at all. After locking the door she moved towards the kitchen. To attract her attention Banka, too, followed her. His Aai and eldest uncle were sitting upon two mats. Auntie went and sat down near them. Banka went near Aai and tugged softly at her pallu but could not muster enough courage to ask for a rasgullah. All his anger was now concentrated on Mother. Mother had become so busy with the women of the village that she did not have any time for him. Why couldn't she keep the key to the storeroom? Since the key was with Auntie she was able to feed her sons rasgullahs whenever she wanted. Why couldn't Mother do that for him? Or was this because she was older in age than Mother? Banka was confused. He thought of asking Grandma for a rasgullah but he felt ashamed to do so before the eldest auntie.

His middle uncle meanwhile joined them and

announced, “I did not find any labourers. I offered them four times the going rate. But still there were no takers.”

“Why did you set up such sophisticated toilets in such a backward rural place?” Aai complained.

“Your daughters and sons-in-law were not visiting the village for want of safety latrines. And now you are complaining. I have been running around in the hot summer to find labourers who will clean the tank of the latrine. The people at the scavengers’ colony are adamant. They say they will not touch the tank with fresh faeces. I looked for labourers to lay new temporary latrines but could not get any. Those rascals would go to far off places as bonded labourers, will go to brick kilns at Hyderabad, but they will not work in the village.” His middle uncle was almost breathless with anger.

Uncle looked after the family’s property. He had not taken up any government job, but nobody had seen him sitting idle even for a moment. He was like a top, always spinning. He never had any time for small talk. But if anyone needed him he would promptly come to their help. Often he came to town with cakes, pickles, and fruits sent by Aai. After blessing the children he would be eager to go back. He was so bashful that he wouldn’t even have a glass of water at his sister’s place.

“But they can’t be blamed. How can you persuade them to clean fresh faeces? The safety tank is completely choked. The new temporary latrine you had set up will brim over in a couple of days. What do you think we should do?” His eldest uncle asked.

"I will clean the tank myself, tomorrow in the morning," Middle Uncle said.

"You will do it?" Aai was startled.

"Yes. The scavengers would have done it. I will do what they would have done. What's the problem? You collect wages eight times the normal rate from your sons-in-law," Middle Uncle joked.

"Can you do it all by yourself?" Eldest Uncle asked.

"Yes, last year two labourers cleaned the tank in two hours. That too they took breaks in between to drink liquor. It is a small tank. Maybe there is some leakage in the plaster from which water is seeping into the tank. Otherwise it would not have filled up in a year's time. When the guests leave, the tank has to be repaired after it is dried properly. This will have to do for now."

"No, no, there are so many relatives. Why should you of all people do this work?" Aai protested.

"What, will I be a lesser human being if I clean the latrine tank? If you look at it that way, well, even Gandhi was a lesser man. What do you say, Banka? You are a good student, they say. Does a human being become less worthy if he does his own work?"

Banka was not ready for such a question. He quickly blurted out, "No."

"Will you clean the tank with me tomorrow?" asked Middle Mama.

"Yes," Banka said, overcoming his reluctance with great difficulty.

"No, no, he is a guest here," Aai remonstrated, "Why are you egging him on? His mother will tear you apart."

Although Banka agreed in a state of confusion, his body shuddered when he contemplated the nature of the work. In town he had seen how scavengers carried the faeces from individual homes in a tin box held atop their heads. He felt like vomiting watching the scene even from a distance. He sometimes wondered how these women collected the faeces of other people in a tin, held like a child in their arm, when even one's own faeces were repulsive to a person. Moreover, while performing that task they were joking among themselves, taking breaks to chew betel nuts and so on. What kind of human beings were they? Were they from a different planet? Why did they submit to such a task? Thank God, there are a set of such beings, otherwise their latrines would have been filled to overflowing in a couple of days, like the tank at Aai's home. Nobody was prepared to undertake the task here despite being offered four times the normal wage. The middle uncle was volunteering to do it himself. Why did he volunteer? Because he was not employed in a government job like his brothers and brothers-in-law? Because he was not highly educated? Why was he asking Banka to be a helping hand? Was it because Banka's father's professional status was lower than that of other relatives? But Banka himself was going to be a great man. He was a good student. He had appeared at the scholarship examination. He would win a scholarship. He would study more. Why should he clean fresh faeces from the latrine tank? His mind was thoroughly disturbed. He decided he would deliberately wake up very late the next morning. Uncle would have cleaned the tank with the help of someone else by that time. Anu bhai, Nanu bhai and Auntie's daughters had been feasting upon tamarind fish and rasgullahs for such a long time. Let them do this work. Why should Banka do it?

He took such a decision in the night, but because of a strong urge to pee Banka woke up from sleep in the wee hours of the morning. After he peed in a remote corner of the compound, he noticed, even through the semi-darkness, his uncle taking out the lid that covered the latrine tank situated near the fencing. He was wearing just a tiny towel around his waist and held a crowbar in his hand. Banka went near him out of curiosity. He realised that Uncle's body was smeared with an oily substance.

"What have you smeared your body with?" asked Banka.

"Kerosene. It will block out the foul smell. Will you join in?"

Banka could not say no. Uncle said, "Remove your shirt and rub kerosene all over your body. Once the work is finished you can bathe, using enough soap to remove the stench of the kerosene. Let me clean the upper layer. Once I get inside the tank, you can carry off the filth I scoop out."

Despite his unwillingness, Banka smeared his body with kerosene kept in a bottle near the well. Uncle was scooping out the watery filth with a small bucket placed outside the tank. While doing so, he was speaking to Banka loudly, "This is your father's, this is your mother's, this is your grandfather's, this is your auntie's... she has swallowed greedily without chewing, and has not been able to digest. Don't you see gobs of clarified butter in the faeces? How can a frog digest clarified butter?"

After half-filling the larger bucket, he held the handle of the bucket with a piece of rug so as not to soil his hand and poured away the contents in one corner of the vegetable garden. Uncle's humorous interjections slowly drove away Banka's initial hatred for the work. One thing, however, still troubled him. How was it that this uncle, who was normally reticent, was cracking so many jokes with him? At home nobody ever talked to him like a friend. Nobody had even sought his help in any work. He was filled with a sense of gratitude for this uncle. There was a surge of devotion in his heart for the man who had volunteered to perform this despicable job so early in the morning when the rest of the family was still in bed, fast asleep. He felt an inner strength in him to help this man.

Uncle then placed his feet on the hinges of the tank wearing a pair of old shoes. He asked Banka to hold two pieces of gunny in his hands. Tying pieces of clean gunny over his palms, Banka held the handle of the bucket, carried it over to the spot Uncle had shown, and poured the contents on the ground. By the time Banka returned, uncle had filled up the other bucket.

Banka held his breath while carrying the bucket. He hated to look at the contents. He poured it on the field that was ploughed recently. After working like this for an hour the task was complete.

By the time the work was done, Banka felt tired. More than the foul smell and the disgust for the putrid, slimy faeces, what troubled him now was the ache in his muscles. And the mild irritation he felt when his sweat mingled with the pungent kerosene. While he was busy cleaning, all the cousins had cast a look at him from a safe distance and then left. In a while Uncle dragged him to the well and helped him take a bath. While rinsing his body with soap, Uncle said, "You know what, Banka, you are a lucky guy. You had a stint in hell very early in your life. Now the rest of your life will be full of the enjoyment of heaven and more heaven. Everyone has to undergo a stint in hell at some point. Even the great king Yudhishthira, the avatar of Dharma and truth, had to dip his little finger in hell before proceeding to heaven. As our body is the abode of both tamarind fish and faeces, so also our lives contain both heaven and hell. But you have to have eyes to see. Now that you saw hell with your own eyes, you will climb up to heaven in your own physical body. You will be a great man when you grow up. Like Mahatma Gandhi or Rishi Dadhichi."

"Mama, I want to be a military man, when I grow up." Banka protested mildly. He believed man went to either heaven or hell when they died. He was not keen to die at this point; rather he was kind of afraid of the idea of death.

Uncle's loud guffaw at his words startled Banka. Uncle said, even as he doubled up in laughter, "Yes, yes you will definitely be a military man. Your training for a military life will begin from tomorrow. Do you see the hill yonder? There is a Hanuman temple on its crest. We will go there tomorrow morning. Your strength to join the military will be tested then."

Banka thought everyone would be full of praise for him because of the service he had rendered in the morning. They would be grateful to him. But although they used both the safety latrines quite comfortably, no one remembered him or Uncle. Only Uncle's wife, the middle auntie, said, while chastising her daughter at lunch, "Foolish girl, why don't you learn a lesson or two from Banka bhai? He is as good in his studies as in his duties." But that was too little, too late to give him any joy. He was looking forward to the thrill Uncle had promised him next morning.

Next day, too, Banka woke up very early. But even then Uncle had already taken his bath and was in the prayer room, immersed in puja. When he saw Banka he said, "Didn't you say you would go to the temple on the hill? Go bathe quickly."

Banka completed his ablutions as soon as possible. He took out a pair of new pants and a new shirt from the suitcase. He put them on even though his body had not dried properly. He set out with uncle. First they went to the plantain grove. Two plants were covered by gunny bags, probably to protect the ripe fruit from being eaten by birds and beasts. Partially removing the gunny bags he extracted a few ripe fruits from the plant. Banka's mouth watered when he saw the size and the ripeness of the fruits which were left to ripen further on the plant itself.

Handing him a banana, he asked, "Want to taste one?"

Banka quickly grabbed the banana and peeled it. "This is the first fruit. It should be offered to Lord Hanuman. And now you have tasted it before the Lord. If your Aai came to know she will curse you. But don't worry, go ahead. After all, you are the child version of Lord Gopala."

While walking alongside his uncle, Banka ate the banana. His stomach was full with just one banana. Uncle asked, "How was it?"

"Good," Banka said.

"Last year, the labourers had deposited the faeces from the tank in the banana orchard. Brinjals will be planted at the place where you dumped the slush yesterday. When you come next year, you will see huge brinjals hanging from the plants there."

With their backs to the sun they were climbing the hill. The rays of the sun were slowly getting hotter. They were leaning forward while climbing on a narrow footpath. By the time they reached the top of the hill Banka was sweating profusely. Uncle, however, was jubilant, singing the Hanuman Chalisa as he climbed. Banka sat down, exhausted, when they reached the temple precincts. Placing the bananas in front of the deity, Uncle gave a loud cry, "Hail, Bajrangbali."

When Banka looked up he saw another huge statue of Hanuman outside the temple as well. The lower portion of the deity was covered with the leaves of a wood apple tree. The deity's chest and head stood two feet taller than the highest branches of the tree. He panicked when he saw the huge deity; he felt as if the Lord himself was standing behind the tree. His head reeled. Uncle asked him, "What happened? Why did you sit down? You are supposed to join the military, aren't you?"

"Uncle, my head is spinning." Banka said weakly.

"Arrey, are you mad or what? You are a young man. And you say your head is spinning?' Uncle hugged him tightly as he said this. Banka felt a little shy. He felt as if Uncle's arms had engulfed the entire horizon. The hill, the temple, the tall Hanuman figure, all had been strung together and contained within those arms. From the reassuring safety of those arms he looked at the village down below. The houses in the village, the date palms, the mango grove, and the human beings appeared too small, like sketches in a drawing book.

Banka asked, "Mama, how is it that Aai's huge house looks so small from here?" At that moment an aeroplane flew past over their heads. Uncle answered, "When you grow up, join the military and fly in an aeroplane, this house, the village, the trees and the human beings will appear even smaller."

# DWARF

*Translated from "Bamana"*

"Yours Affectionately Banka."

After finishing the letter according to the formula taught by the teacher in the letter-writing class, Banka Harichandan glanced through it again quickly. The word "Affectionately" seemed to him somewhat incongruous. The word did not jell with whatever he had written in the letter; rather it seemed to dilute the anger he had tried to express. So he crossed out the last line. He scratched out those three words so many times that nobody could guess what was initially written. Then below that crossed out line he wrote in a slightly bolder font, "Yours Banka Harichandan".

He then assured himself that all letters need not be written in a run-of-the-mill fashion. Moreover, he had hopes of becoming a writer when he grew up. How could he become a writer unless he wrote something new by breaking old formulas?

His mind was in a throb, much like itchy scabs on the thigh on their way to healing. He wrote the letter, giving vent to all his feelings freely like a great writer, but would he be able to face the consequence? In fact, for a few moments he was really delighted by the words of the letter which expressed his anger, irritation and frustration in such an exquisite manner. If Alok read it he would like to tear out his own hair and kill himself. But what if he did not do that?

What if he showed the letter to the teachers instead? If he showed it to Nanda Sir who taught literature, he would definitely admire it. Nanda Sir was very caring about him. Once in a while he had this habit of proclaiming to the entire class that this boy Banka would become a writer when he grew up. He sometimes read his literature answer scripts aloud in the class, hailing them as model answers. Partly because of him Banka had reckoned being a writer was his life's aim. If Nanda Sir read the letter aloud in the tenth class? The matter would be public. Nani would come to know about it. If she knew, Chacha would know too. He would beat him to jelly. She would also feel humiliated. If out of shame she, too, like the woman who lived as a tenant at Sati's house, decided to.... Oh, Bajrangbali.... Banka could think no further. He tore up the letter hurriedly and threw the bits of paper in the backyard.

Now he tore off another page from the rough notebook and sat down to write afresh. This time too, he was helped along by his own command of language and artistry in weaving words together. Again he was impressed by his own letter. He was convinced that all the possibilities of a future writer were packed in him. How effortlessly he emptied out all the anger, irritation and frustration of the previous letter! In their place he could lace the new words with adequate mockery, satire and scorn. He also discovered another element in the new letter; the sentences were so slanted that anyone unaware of the context would not be able to make much of it. He had cited such examples that close friends would be foxed. It might be that even Alok himself would not be able to understand much of it. He was an ass in matters of studies. How could he make out the full import of the letter? But he could surely make out that he had been mocked in the letter. But then he might not be in a position to show the letter to any teacher. Just because his father happened to be a high official the teachers never reprimanded him openly, but they must be irritated with him internally, for the teachers were normally impatient with stupid students. He certainly would not be able to show his teachers a letter that was so meaningless and rambling.

He might not be able to complain before the teachers, but that didn't mean he couldn't throw down the gauntlet on his critics. The well-built, hefty figure of Alok flashed across Banka's mind's eye. Let alone junior boys, Alok was capable of fouling older students at football matches. It was only due to him that their class became the champions of the football tournament every year. Players were afraid of tackling him when he manned the goal-area as the full-back of their team. If anybody dared to do so during the game Alok beat them up badly after the match was over. If Alok beat him up after getting the letter? What could he do? Even the teachers never rebuked him because of his high-ranking father. Rather when the entire episode came to light, he would face the music at home for nobody ever tried to understand him.

Banka regretted befriending Alok in the first place. But, of course, he had not made the first move. It was Alok who had forced himself on him. Otherwise how would he have dared to be close to somebody who studied three classes above him, with Nani? Two hefty men brought Alok's lunch-box in a car during the mid-day break. One of them was his driver and the other was a peon in his father's office. Both of them tried to feed him somehow, tolerating all his tantrums, in the car which they parked at a little distance from the school playground. On a few occasions Banka had watched the whole farce from a distance along with other students. Unlike Alok, Banka and other students did not have access to the luxury of mid-day meals. They used to have their meals before school hours commenced at ten a.m. and had to wait for their next meal after school at four o'clock. At times, when Banka returned home the plate of rice was the only thing that held his interest in life. It was a matter of great surprise for him that Alok threw away most of the food brought for him and abused the attendants in full public view. On one such occasion, when Banka was watching him from a distance with surprise, Alok asked him to come closer. When his other friends like Danei and Krupa tagged along, Alok waved them off rudely, "I called him, not you rascals."

After they took to their heels in fright, Alok asked Banka to sit down beside him in his car. Banka felt comfortable on the soft cushion of the car seat. When he inhaled the smell of the perfume in the car's interior mingled with the aroma of chicken biryani emanating from the tiffin-carrier, his hunger, subdued for ages, leapt up like the fire in a yajna at the offering of ghee. Sometimes the smell of biryani being cooked at Piru Mian's shop enchanted him like this on his way back from school. When he stopped on the path to inhale the aroma coming from the shop, he heard Nani's reprimand, "Hey, loafer, don't you feel like going home? Hurry up." Perforce he had to clutch his school bag tightly across his chest and follow her at a quickened trot.

When Alok held up the tiffin-box to him that day, he felt as if his heart had stopped beating. He was debating whether he should accept or turn down the offer, when Alok's peon cajoled, "Master, you also have a helping." Alok shouted him down, "Shut up. Who are you to tell me what I do with my food? Wait, I am going to report at home about you. I had asked you to bring mutton-biryani and you have got me chicken?"

"Master, I am sorry. I will cook mutton tomorrow definitely. Have something to eat today. What will I say to your mother?"

"You just tell Mum that I ate heartily, it was so good. Or else, I will ask Papa to stop your salary. Banka, you eat."

Banka was terribly confused by this exchange of words. When Alok shot out his instructions he started gulping down the food without giving any thought to the consequences. He was hardly aware of the taste of the food he was eating. This, then, was chicken-biryani? He was unable to match the object with the sweet smell that wafted down from Piru Mian's shop. Probably, he was not able to appreciate the taste because it was offered by Alok. Who knows?

It became a part of his daily routine after that day. Alok would invariably invite him during lunch-break to share his meal. Lest his elder sister should come to know and report him at home, they would drive a little distance away from school and enjoy their meal together. They would return to their respective classrooms as if nothing unusual had happened when they were away together. Although Nani did not know about the development, his classmates were aware of Alok's soft corner for Banka. They didn't take liberties with him anymore. The usual teasing, like squeezing his bottom, kissing his cheeks or imitating the act of drawing milk from his chest by sucking on his nipples stopped abruptly. Once when Chaina embraced Banka from behind Alok punched his back so hard that he could not come to school for a couple of days. After that incident his classmates became scared of bullying Banka. This was a welcome change for Banka who never enjoyed the acts of bullying but did not protest out of fear, or inform his teachers lest the issue get out of hand and people at home get to know and his mother and Chacha blame him for everything without checking the facts. And a thrashing would follow. After Alok befriended him all his troubles seemed to have ended. On top of that, there was a divine meal every day.

But who could stop Kurupa, the rascal? Once Alok was absent from school and Banka was roaming alone during the lunch-break. Kurupa asked him, “Are you on the lookout for your bhinei?”

Banka at first could not understand the question at all. He just stared at Kurupa’s face blankly.

“Your sister’s husband, your brother-in-law? He is going to marry her. That’s why he is feeding you every day.”

Banka was terribly enraged. “Shall I report to the teachers that you are calling me names?” Banka growled.

“Please do. I will also let your sister know how you are running after Alok like a beggar for a share in his snack. Why does it irk you so, when you are told the truth?” Kurupa’s threat restrained Banka from bringing the matter to the notice of the teachers.

But the next day he took Alok into confidence, “Alok bhai, Kurupa is spreading nasty lies linking you with my sister.”

He expected Alok to get angry and teach Kurupa a bitter lesson. But what the hell! Instead of getting angry, Alok merely smiled a little and was silent.

As days passed by, other boys too joined in teasing Banka, “Hello ‘sala’, how are you doing today?” Alok had not chastised Kurupa at being called bhinei, so how could Banka have complained to him that he was being called "sala", the term for a wife's brother? Moreover, Banka observed that Alok, who used to get angry at small provocations, seemed to enjoy this sobriquet of sala. With Alok's silent encouragement the boys began to tease Banka more and more. Now he had misgivings. Was it true that Alok's liking for him was really a cover for his liking for Nani? Was his sharing of meals a ploy to attract her attention?

Sometimes Banka felt like asking Alok directly to resolve his doubts. Or maybe he would refuse to accompany him during lunch-breaks. But he was also mortally afraid of Alok's anger. Moreover, the bullies of his class had been silenced because of Alok's friendship. If he forsook his company they would tease him with redoubled vigour. He felt trapped. Though he accompanied Alok during lunch-breaks as usual, he felt like he was choking on the food he offered him. He kept on cursing himself for accepting his invitation in the first place. Now the truth of his mother's advice cascaded over him with full force. Mother had strictly instructed him not to take anything from anyone. And to be truthful. Always. Now he was unable to confront Alok with the truth because he had shared his meals. On the other hand, the fact Alok was offering him food with an ulterior motive pained him no end. He silently resolved to give up all temptations and fear. He had to tell the truth, otherwise how could he become a writer when he grew up?

At last, one day, gathering all his courage after reading

the Hanuman Chalisa one hundred and eight times, he confronted Alok during the lunch-break. "Brother, I cannot accompany you during lunch-breaks anymore." As he uttered these words, he burst into tears with fear, shame and anxiety.

His tears completely unsettled even a hulk like Alok. "Why, what happened?" he asked. Still weeping, Banka said, "If my sister comes to know, she will spill the beans at home." Alok was reassured, "Oh! This? Nothing will happen. How would she know? If anyone dares to inform your sister I'll grind their bones into powder. Do you know I love your sister?"

Alok said this ostensibly to assuage his apprehensions but Banka felt as if someone had plunged a crowbar into his chest. Forget about his sobbing, Alok's words almost stopped his breathing. What he feared most was true after all? Kurupa, Chaina, and the others were telling the truth, then? The real reason Alok was so chummy with him was his elder sister? How badly he wished to pluck out Alok's eyes with the divider from his geometry box and stab him all over his body! He could accomplish his task before Alok had time to react! But sighting Alok's driver with a long moustache and the peon adjusting a towel over his shoulder, he expelled the idea from his mind.

Fear made him go completely silent. Alok, however, was persisting with his request. "Don't tell your sister, please. I will give you the Parker pen my father gave me recently."

Alok's words were now inaudible to him. He quickly escaped into his classroom. An overwhelming sense of shame and humiliation had blocked all sounds from reaching his ear-drums. A rush of blood made his face feel warm. Sitting in the front row of the class, he had opened his literature textbook during a geometry class. Fortunately, it escaped the attention of the teacher, or he would have landed himself in more trouble.

Banka glanced at Pushpa sitting on a nearby bench out of the corner of his eyes. But he did not feel the usual elation at the sight of her. Rather, a sense of guilt overtook him that day for this furtive action. He somehow regained his equilibrium only when the school closed for the day. On normal days Banka used to follow his sister while returning home. She walked ahead and he followed her leisurely, chatting with his classmates. That day, he hurriedly walked home without heeding her. He washed his feet and hands and sat down for the afternoon meal. But he was not in a position to relish the food he shoved in his mouth. An overwhelming sense of discomfort occupied him. Nothing was interesting to him. The memory of Alok's words kept piercing his face like needles. He was unable to muster enough courage to look his sister in the eye. He went to the nearby playground so that he could avoid her for some time, but even there, there was no comfort. The stray thoughts linking Alok with his sister kept troubling him. Maybe he would have found some peace if he had actually pierced Alok's eyes with a divider. But how could he have done so to a bull like Alok? "O Bajrangbali make me a grown-up at once," he prayed pitifully. If his physique could be like that of the simian god somehow, he would definitely thrash Alok from top to bottom as he helplessly rolled across the school playground.

But could he have beaten up Alok mercilessly as he desired? The meals he had shared, the places he had taken him to in his luxury car in the last three or four months, would that not have restrained him, even if he had the demonic strength to beat him up? But why bother about such futile thoughts. There was no way the simian god was going to give him that demonic strength or turn him into a grown-up. Had the god ever fulfilled any of his prayers so far? All gods are like homeopathic medicine; in real crisis they are useless. Even if the simian god did not turn him into a fully-grown man, could he at least not kill Alok with some kind of disease? Or maybe make a car accident happen. This should be easy. It would not take a lot for the simian god to accomplish this much! As he was on the verge of praying accordingly, a sense of guilt flashed across his mind. Should he make such an evil prayer? Every morning before leaving the bed he prayed, "let everyone be happy, let them all be free of any illness" and so on, reciting the Vedic mantra in Sanskrit, of course, out of fear of Father's beating. But he felt nice after the prayer. True, one would feel good if everyone was happy. Was it nice to think ill of someone? Just because Alok said something unpalatable, would he go so far as to wish his death? Moreover, he himself loved

Pushpa. He was scared to tell this to Pushpa directly, but, what if Pushpa's younger brother prayed to god for his death? And if god really granted all human prayers, then what? Alok would die, but he too would have to die along with him.

Banka was totally confused. Expelling all the thoughts about gods and goddesses, he returned home early. Alok had not said anything so bad that it should breed such deep rancour in him, he assured himself. Love, after all, is not a bad thing. But still, he was unable to imagine Alok with his sister. If it was not a bad thing, why was he so distraught? His agitation hovered during the evening prayer like a cloud in the sky. It even lingered into dinner time. His favourite dish, cauliflower curry, which he never hesitated to take several helpings of, felt tasteless. Feigning drowsiness he went to bed early but sleep eluded him. He ended up tossing and turning on the bed for a long time. Though sleep overtook him eventually, terrifying nightmares interrupted again and again. And whenever he woke up, thoughts about Alok and his sister barged into his consciousness.

After deciding to write the letter on Sunday morning he felt somewhat easy. With the letter he had planned to communicate what he had failed to express in either action or speech in such a manner that Alok would never repeat the mistake in his entire lifetime. He also took a vow that he too would not harbour the thought of loving Pushpa anymore. Though he had spent the entire evening fashioning the letter, he was unable to finish writing it. After four false starts, Banka realised that there was no language which could crush Alok without putting himself at risk. Each time after completing a draft of the letter he felt he could not wash his hands off whatever hurt the letter might cause Alok. On the contrary, the more the hurt to Alok the more the danger to himself. After rejecting the fourth draft, he finally decided that he would not write the letter at all. After all, Alok had not uttered anything that was abominable. Moreover, whatever he had said was meant for his sister. Why should he bother so much about her? Did she even love him? Rather she always rebuked him. Threatened to tell on him to Chacha. Banka stopped writing the letter. Pulled out a dictionary and opened the lesson of his literature textbook which was supposed to be taught the next day.

Once he opened the book the image of the woman who rented Sati's house flashed across his mind. He had gone to Harish's place one morning. On the way Harish told him, "I shall show you a wonderful sight. The woman who lived in our neighbour Sati's house has hanged herself. Police must have reached by now. Come, there will be a lot of fun."

He had accompanied Harish, hoping to expel the thought of Alok which had been troubling him, but he didn't want to go along when he heard about the suicide. "No, I don't like to see dead bodies," he said.

"Are you a nincompoop or what? Why don't you tell me directly that you are scared? 'I don't like,' what does that mean? Wait, I will declare tomorrow at school what a coward you are. Bloody eunuch, what kind of a writer are you planning to become?" Harish fired his ultimate salvo.

Whenever Banka refused his bidding Harish used this weapon. According to him, anyone who wanted to become a writer had to smoke bidis. He had to fill a condom with water, tie its head with a thread and play with it. Harish's chacha was a great writer, he was known to indulge in these things when he was a kid. When he grew up and actually became a writer, he started drinking alcohol. Harish had also promised to give him a taste of alcohol at some point before he became a writer.

When Banka reached Sati's place with Harish, a large crowd had already gathered there. In the inner courtyard of the house, Sati's mother was whimpering along with her daughter. She was scared the police would take her husband away. The police jeep arrived immediately after they reached there. As soon as the officer alighted from the vehicle two constables who were loitering there ran up to him and saluted. The officer expressed his displeasure, "Why is there such a crowd? Are we staging a street play here?"

The two constables immediately shooed away the crowd gathered there. Standing upon Harish's veranda they were able to witness the scene in Sati's courtyard. Once the crowd left, they could see the corpse clearly. She was a heavy woman. The saree she had used as a knot for hanging was still attached to her neck. The havildar, accompanying the officer, was scribbling something in a notebook. Suddenly the officer shouted, "What, are you uncomfortable in front of a dead body? Such squeamishness on the part of a policeman?"

The constable advanced a few steps after the reprimand but retreated immediately. He pulled out a handkerchief and tied it around his face and resumed his advance towards the dead body. Banka's patience was at an end.

"I am leaving. My chacha might have returned from the market. I have not worked on my sums."

Harish flaunted his courage earlier, but now he did not restrain Banka.

"Let me walk you down to your home." On their way Harish told him, "Don't you know that woman was pregnant. The young man for whom she left her home deserted her. They had been living here for a couple of months."

Banka had felt like vomiting after hearing Harish's account. When he remembered the incident of that morning, he immediately closed his book, yanked a page out from his rough notebook and resolutely began writing the letter.

His mother turned up around the same time. "Are you studying or reading some story book?"

Once he had been caught reading a story book, carefully hidden within the belly of a textbook.

"I am practising my letter-writing. The teacher has assigned this homework." Banka responded with great displeasure. "Let me see," Mother extended her hand for the piece of paper on which Banka was going to write.

"Oh! Bless me! You are running a fever it seems. What do I do with such a child? You recovered from fever only the other day. Go, go to bed at once. No school for you tomorrow. I will give you a dose of alkasol after dinner." Mother went back to the kitchen mumbling inaudibly.

She was right: Banka's body felt as if it was on fire by that time. He had planned to write the letter and hand it over to Alok the next day at school, but the way things were shaping up he would not be able to go to school. While he was thinking about how to pass the letter to Alok, a novel idea struck him. When Harish would come the next day to accompany him to school, he would put the letter inside his school bag, for Harish would be scared to hand-deliver the letter to Alok. When Harish would open his bag, he would definitely notice the letter addressed to Alok and give it to him. But he would have to keep the letter in Harish's bag stealthily so that he would not know. But what if it slipped Harish's eyes and the letter remained undelivered? Well, let him not get the letter. At least Banka would have the satisfaction of completing his part of the duty. After consoling himself with this thought he wrote a one-liner in bold handwriting on the page he had yanked out

**A DWARF SHOULD NEVER ASPIRE TO REACH THE MOON.**

A one-line letter, without the address of the sender or the receiver, and, which, therefore, fell outside of the formula the teacher had taught in the letter-writing class. With such a letter he of course succeeded in averting all kinds of risk to himself but went to bed with a great sense of dissatisfaction. When he grew up, he might at best be a poet, but not a writer, he reckoned.

# FIRST SEPARATION

*Translated from "Pratham Biraha"*

It was from Sati's mother that Banka first heard about the new neighbours. She came on Sunday afternoons when everybody enjoyed their siesta and filled Mother in on the stories of the week.

"Many times I plan to come but I cannot even find time to die", she says and opens her casket of stories. In those moments Mother and Sati's mother turn into two companions. Sati's mother, who earns her living doing odd jobs in different homes, does not consider herself inferior; nor does Mother consider herself superior to her maidservant's mother. Rather, on those weekend afternoons Sati's mother brings a glimpse of a wider world to Mother, who lives within the four walls of the house, buffeted by the demands of in-laws and young children. On those afternoons she no longer remains the mother of the maid servant. Not that Nani does not try to claim a share in their gossip. But Mother turns her away with a reprimand, "Why are you butting into a conversation between adults? Go do your work. The music teacher will turn up in a little while."

Nani is foolish, Banka thinks. Where is the need to get up from bed and glue yourself to her if you want to hear Sati's mother? Why invite Mother's rebuke? Banka remains in the bed, feigning sleep, his ears riveted to the ongoing conversation. Lapping up the deepest secrets of the mystery Sati's mother reeled out. Sati's mother might think that she was whispering those secrets only for the benefit of Mother's ears and not for others, but her voice was such that even at its lowest pitch the entire locality could hear what she was saying. Only one should not be a fool like Nani.

"The haunted house is finally rented out, I hear."

"Yes. A ghost has occupied it," answered Sati's mother and giggled, impressed by her own sense of humour. "The man looks so horrid that even ghosts would be scared of him. What fear of ghosts he would have? But the wife is a beauty. Better to look at her than the statue of goddess Durga during the annual Puja. She is as beautiful as she is young. Her parents must be butchers. Otherwise how could they hand over such a young beauty to this vile-looking old haggard? Moreover, she is the old man's second wife."

"They might be poor. Marrying off a girl is such an expensive affair these days," Mother said, in a show of sympathy for the unknown parents of the woman.

"One would like to believe that the man would be serving meals to her on a golden plate? But no, he has taken the haunted house for its low rent."

No tenant lived for long in that house that bore

the infamy of being haunted. The house owner was a Bengali man from Kolkata. He visited his property only infrequently. When he did, he stayed for a couple of days in a room upstairs that otherwise remained locked up. Then he would go on his usual trip to Puri. The huge garden surrounding the house fell prey to the tyranny of local urchins for the rest of the period. The garden also catered to the sundry needs of the entire locality. The neighbourhood boys polished off the mangoes, jackfruits, star apples, and lichi fruits that grew abundantly in the garden in their respective seasons. Disputes and skirmishes were known to break out among local women who frequented the garden to collect firewood for their kitchen and fresh grass for their cattle.

Mother said the owner had appointed a caretaker to tend the garden and look after the house, but he left due to the fear of ghosts. No one had come to replace him so far. The place had fallen into neglect and lost its sheen. It was now purely at the mercy of occasional tenants who too did not stay long despite the falling rent. But Faka, the son of the shopkeeper, said this talk of ghosts was sheer cock and bull; he said Chheta, Godhi and the other neighbourhood wastrels had spread this rumour. Whenever a new tenant came in these rascals resorted to throwing stones and faeces at the house every night, and made weird sounds to scare the poor tenants away.

An empty house suited them perfectly, its huge veranda serving as a place for their nocturnal addas. There they drank beer and alcohol, smoked hemp and had a romp with loose women. Banka had heard about hemp and liquor. On the way to school he had stealthily smoked bidis with Faka, who had explained to him that the thrill of liquor and hemp was a hundred times more than the kick of bidi. Banka was scared. He was already at his wit's end, swallowing bidi-smoke. A thrill that was a hundred times more than that was simply unimaginable for him. But Faka had not explained what a romp was. He just let him know that it was a ride that was super good, a lot of "masti". You had to have a proper build up with liquor and hemp in order to enjoy that "masti", the supreme pleasure. The feeling of "masti" must cut extraordinarily deep, otherwise why should anybody endure the tyranny of alcohol and hemp which was a hundred times more painful than the smoke of bidi? But why did Faka not explain this thing called "masti" properly? The rascal just made a false promise that he would do so later. Probably he himself did not know. If he had never had a romp with a woman, how would he know? To know the meaning of "masti" Banka consulted two to three dictionaries from his father's book-rack. But the word itself did not exist in any one of them. Further, Banka knew that there was a difference of heaven and hell between the meaning of a word and the experience to which that word beckoned.

"Don't they have children?" Banka heard his mother asking Sati's mother.

"Two. A boy and a girl." Sati's mother whispered, apparently lowering her voice, which could of course be heard by a person walking on the main street. "A boy of fourteen or fifteen from the first wife. A girl of nine or ten from this woman. Not a girl, you had better call her an angel from heaven. Takes after her mother. The same betel-leaf like face, the same beautiful eyes, and skin colour the same mix of milk and honey..."

A peculiar tumult seized Banka's chest. He could no longer hear what else Sati's mother was describing. His chest felt choked, and he was sweating profusely, although he was lying closest to the table-fan. His heart was thumping inside his chest like the threshing-horse in Aai's courtyard in the village. He felt as if something inside him was desperately flailing around in order to escape his body and spread out across the sky. The impulse to fly out filled his mind with as much joy as the fear of not being able to return to the body paralysed his entire being.

A sudden light flooded Banka's consciousness. Probably this simultaneous feeling of joy and fear was "masti". And this was a forbidden experience that was obtained in great secrecy, away from the eyes of the world. For this reason Chheta, Godhi and their ilk had their romps in the dead of the night in an abandoned and haunted house. For this reason Chacha was beaten by Father while reading the Mastram book which he had kept hidden inside his college book. For this reason Sonali didi had once pressed his mouth to her breasts while tightly embracing him behind the closed doors of her room. When Banka felt breathless under her embrace and struggled to free himself she had given him a huge Cadbury chocolate and said, "Don't tell anybody you were in my room. I will give you more chocolates."

Banka felt extremely relieved after escaping Sonali didi's clutches. Licking on his chocolate he returned home like a king after a royal visit. He wanted the whole world to witness that he was feasting on such an expensive chocolate entirely by himself. He reached home driven by the pride of this achievement, but Nani, who had the ability to pull the rug from under all his triumphs, shouted out from somewhere, "Mother, this glutton is eating a chocolate he has begged from someone."

Banka had to do a lot of explaining. He had to swear before Mother that he had not begged; that, in fact, Sonali didi had forced the chocolate on him. She also showed her appreciation because he had stood first in the class exam. "She has promised to give more if I study well," Banka lied. But Mother was determined. She admonished him, "If you feed on a policeman's corrupt money your body will be poisoned. You will forget whatever you studied so diligently. Your intelligence will be lost. There are no young boys in their house. Why are you running to their house, like an effeminate idiot, to play with grown-up girls much older than you? You swear by the name of god that you will never cross the threshold of Satpathy uncle's house again."

Banka had to touch the photograph of the simian god Hanuman and swear in his name. He had not gone to Satpathy uncle's house after that day. His attraction for chocolate might have easily overcome the fear he had developed for Sonali didi after her embrace, but Mother had already convinced him that even when nobody was watching you, Hanuman had the ability to see everything everywhere anytime. Since he had taken a vow after touching Hanuman's photo he had not been able to marshal enough courage to visit Sonali didi's house again.

But on hearing from Sati's mother about the nine-to ten-year-old girl who was prettier than even her beautiful mother he took a silent vow to cross the threshold of the haunted house. He was convinced that the experience of "masti" would not be available to him in any dictionary; rather the haunted house held the possibility for such an experience. He made an elaborate plan to acquire that experience.

First, he controlled his heart which was beating furiously like a threshing-horse. Then he dedicated a prayer to the simian god Lord Hanuman as he usually did before all his important actions. In addition, he promised a huge bunch of plantains as an offering to the Lord if he succeeded in his mission. He got up from the sleeping mat and hurriedly gulped down two glasses of water from the pitcher. By then Sati's mother was engaged in daily household chores and Mother had repaired to the kitchen to make tea. Lest Father should wake up due to the disturbance, he did not pick up his cricket bat and left home quietly through the back door and headed towards the playground. Other players had not reached there by that time. He waited beneath a neem tree near the ground. After some time, Faka, the shopkeeper's son, brandishing two wooden sticks like swords, descended on the field, his younger brother Makara following him with a tennis ball in his hand.

Sighting him from a distance, Faka hollered, "Hey, where is the bat?'

"Father has locked it up in the store-room because examinations are in the offing. He will let me take it out only after the examination," Banka lied.

"What bloody exam you are barking about? The semester exam ended only a couple of days ago!" Faka, who had the least contact with studies, expressed his displeasure.

"You don't understand. Father is so unreasonable, you know. It is so tough to make him understand any damn thing. I will somehow placate Mother and bring the bat tomorrow when Father goes away on an official tour. Let's take a stroll around the haunted house this afternoon."

"The haunted house is already on rent. Has been for three to four months. You don't know? Some bloody moron lives there now. If he gets hold of you, you'll be screwed. What an idea! 'Take a stroll around the haunted house,' an idea really! On other occasions when I asked you to go there, you always chickened out. With all kinds of alibis. Today I have homework to finish. Tomorrow the tutor will come. Now that we have turned up for cricket practice this fool says to go to the haunted house. Tell me the reason for your newfound love for the haunted house." Faka was visibly annoyed. "Don't you remember we have a match with the team of the neighbouring sahi next week?"

Then he instructed his younger brother, "Makara, go and fetch the spare bat from home. We will continue our practice." Then he proceeded to fix the sticks on the ground which would serve as wickets.

Banka's enthusiasm waned. But still, intoxicated by the image of the beautiful young girl described by Sati's mother, he slowly crossed the ground and was willy-nilly drawn towards the house located at the farthest corner of their locality. His tension had somewhat subsided. The absence of Faka, who had saved him from many a danger by his ready wit, had made him a bit diffident. But when from a distance he saw Satpathy uncle in his full police uniform sitting on a chair on the veranda of the haunted house, he felt as if someone had doused all his enthusiasm with a huge bucket of cold water. Silently he cursed Satpathy uncle, Sonali didi and their entire clan to his heart's content and offered a bribe of another bunch of bananas to the simian god. "O, Bajrangbali, please burn the entire clan to ashes."

Just at that moment, seeing Banka hovering around the main gate of the house, Satpathy uncle called out, "Hey Banka, why are you loitering there, why don't you come in?"

Perforce Banka had to open the gate and enter the yard. As he approached the veranda Satpathy uncle introduced him to the person Faka had called a moron, "He is our neighbour Mr. Mohapatra's son. Mr. Mohapatra is a fine gentleman. This boy is also very bright. He always receives merit scholarships for his studies. Like father, like son."

The moron was smiling approvingly. His sparkling rows of white teeth, making a contrast with the face, dark like a burnt kettle, made his smile hideous. He wore a blue lungi tied around his waist and a sleeveless vest. The vest, however, was unable to hide the thick bunch of grey hair on his arms and chest. A short distance away, near the threshold of the front door and holding the door screen, stood the beautiful young woman so neatly described by Sati's mother. And covering half of her face and a part of her body behind her mother's pallu stood the girl for whom Banka had embarked on his mission.

But when Banka's eyes met hers, the girl smiled at him and ran inside, letting go of her mother's pallu. The sight of her evanescing frock was almost like a scorpion sting that released a generous dose of venom into his blood stream. Although Mother had not opened up about this before, Banka realised that, apart from money corruptly earned, there were a thousand other things in this world, capable of making your heart race like mad, as though from a whiplash of venom. He also realised that poison after all was not a bad or dangerous thing always. This particular poison was so alluring that one would not be scared to drown in it despite the threat of being killed.

"Arrey, come in. Why are you standing out there

in the yard? Are you feeling shy? What class are you studying in? Our son is around, come inside. Babu, here is a new friend. Ask him in." The moron was going on and on. But nothing was registering in Banka's mind. He was not willing to share the thrill of the new poison with Babu or any Rama, Bhima and Shama. He was trying his best to preserve till eternity the memory of that smile and the whiplash of that receding frock. Lest that memory should get diluted if there were other distractions, he hurriedly bade goodbye. "Uncle, I will come some other time. I have a lot of studying to do this evening."

Saying this somehow, Banka quickly crossed the yard of the haunted house and exited on to the street. His entire body was drenched with perspiration. His chest had again started beating like a threshing horse. With a profound peace settled on his consciousness, he had gone past the usual feeling of fear, agitation and joy. He felt a sense of identity with the entire world. A strange feeling of empathy emanated from him for the ugly-looking moron, his beautiful young wife, the corrupt police officer Satpathy uncle, the asphyxiating embrace of Sonali didi, and even the mischief mongering and romping sessions of Chheta and Godhi. During that moment of empathy he offered a prayer to the simian god Hanuman, "O Lord Bajrangbali, let Sati's mother live long. Grant millions of years of lifetime to Mother, Father, Nani, Chacha, and everyone else."

Days passed by. It was Sunday again. The scorching heat of the afternoon brought Mother, the mistress of the house, and the mother of the servant-maid Sati to the same sealed space. They sat down with their faces close to each other, having banished foolish Nani from the world of their whispering tales. Feigning sleep Banka kept his ears riveted to their exchange. Banka's enthusiasm for the box of tales of Sati's mother had increased manifold. By this time Banka had realised why adults indulged in gossiping and back-biting, although there was no immediate benefit to be had from that. Whether Mother benefitted in any way or not from this, it had transformed Banka's entire life wonderfully.

"The police babu is visiting the haunted house at odd hours. People's tongues have started to wag," Sati's mother confided.

"People seem to have no work of their own. So what if somebody visited someone's house? They can go wherever they like. Should he have asked prior permission from them before visiting? The person whose house he is visiting is not complaining. Why are others so upset?" Mother said, hoping by her nudges to ferret out the whole story from Sati's mother.

"The problem is elsewhere, Banka's Mother!" Although Nani was elder, a mother feels prouder to be called the mother of a male child and Sati's mother was the only one who addressed her as Banka's mother. "Now the wife of Satpathy babu has come to know about it. There has been a lot of friction between the husband and the wife over this."

"What is so new about it? Your Mrs. Satpathy is such

a shrew. She is always spoiling for a fight. Just because she is the wife of the local police station in-charge she has airs, one foot above the ground. There is a high tide of fish and goat-meat curry entering their house every day, supported by ill-got money. Why the fuss now?" Mother tried to provoke.

"The water has risen to such heights now and you are asking what is the fuss, Banka's dear mother? After enquiries the officer-in-charge learnt that these hooligans, Chheta and Godhi, were throwing stones at the haunted house in the dead of the night. He rounded them up at the police station for interrogation. His wife showed up there herself and freed them from police custody. Now those loafers have been adopted by her as her godsons. They are bloody criminals already, now they have the patronage of Mrs. Satpathy. Will their nuisance decrease or increase? If you do not trust my words, why don't you ask Banka. He has befriended the boy from the haunted house of late."

A peculiar tumult seized his chest when Banka heard her last few words. His heart started thumping like the threshing horse. He could no longer hear what other news Sati's mother was reeling out. Despite the full speed of the table-fan his body started sweating profusely in anticipation of some unknown catastrophe. But Banka was clear in his mind that these symptoms were the exact opposite of the feeling of "masti". In these there was only unreasonable fear and anxiety. There was no trace of the joyous freedom which "masti" supposedly bestowed.

When Sati's mother went out to attend to the chores, Banka got up from the mat in great haste and gulped down a full glass of water which he had poured from the earthenware pitcher. When he felt a little comforted after some time he heard Mother's voice. In a cajoling manner she asked, "Banka, does the boy of the haunted house play with you?"

Despite Mother's amiable tone, Banka's entire body shook with fright. His voice was choked. With great difficulty he responded haltingly, "Why, no. I do not know him at all. I swear by the name of god. If you do not believe me why don't you cross-check with Faka and Makara." After he blurted this out, he realised that by giving such an elaborate answer to Mother's seemingly innocent question he had unnecessarily dragged himself into the zone of suspicion.

"It is alright. Playing together is not such a bad thing. But never go to their house. Probably there are ghosts in that house who throw stones during the night. But what do ghosts know? Why can't they throw a stone or two during daytime also, especially to scare a young boy like you?"

"I will never cross their threshold," Banka assured his mother and left for the playground with bat in hand. He was apprehensive that Mother would extract a similar vow from him, holding the photograph of the simian god Lord Hanuman as witness, which would completely destroy the possibility of his having a look at the young frock-clad beauty forever. The cherished zone of "masti" would forever be beyond his reach, as had been Sonali didi's Cadbury chocolates of late.

Of course, his first sighting of the girl had been his last. After that, on his way back from school, he had hovered around the haunted house several times while playing cricket; but he had not been able to muster enough courage to enter the premises. Faka had always parried his proposal to visit the haunted house with some alibi or the other. He had also not been successful in befriending Babu, the haunted house boy, after several attempts. The boy was such a sour-faced loner that he had flatly denied his proposal to be a part of their team in a cricket match. But still, by repeatedly remembering the girl's smile that day and the poison her vanishing frock had injected into him, Banka had died several deaths and had been brought back to life again and again. For this "masti" of dying and having a new lease of life Banka had been drawn towards the haunted house over and over.

But that day he reached the playground with the final determination of crossing the threshold of the house. Setting up three ramshackle sticks as stumps, Faka, Makara and the others had already begun their cricket practice with a tennis ball and a piece of flattened wood for a bat. The match with the neighbouring sahi was coming up. Banka was greeted with an enthusiastic chorus when he was sighted. "Look, the bat has arrived."

After handing over the bat to Makara, he led Faka to the neem tree. He said to Faka in a begging voice, "Faka, let them play. Meanwhile, why don't we go for a stroll around the haunted house."

"What nonsense! We have the match coming up. Instead of practising hard, this fool suggests a stroll around the haunted house! Don't you remember we were defeated in the last match only because of you? This time around we must take revenge. No compromise." Faka spoke angrily, imitating the style of Chheta and Godhi. After a few moments, lowering his voice considerably, Faka again said, "Are you angling for the daughter of that moron? Why are you repeatedly uttering the name of the haunted house like someone possessed?"

Although the clothes he was wearing hadn't slipped off his body, Banka felt as if he was standing completely naked in front of Faka. And Faka was reading his soul with the same ease with which Sankar Sir solved difficult mathematical problems in class.

"Hey shut up. Babu is a very good batsman. I wanted you to persuade him to play for our team. But if you have such rotten ideas about me, I don't feel like playing in your team."

"We don't care, man. You think you are some Gavaskar or what! We don't care two hoots about your playing and we don't give a damn to your not playing either." Faka was carried away by the force of the argument.

"Is this your final wish?" Banka challenged.

"Yes. Final. Final. Final."

"Okay," blurted out Banka and snatched his expensive cricket bat from Makara's hand and ran home without a single backward glance. As the owner of the only legitimate cricket bat, his stature in his own team as well as in the team of the neighbouring sahi was very high. Banka knew that without his bat no cricket match between the sahis could ever be contemplated. Although Faka had spoken in that manner in the heat of the moment, he knew what all these assholes would have said after he left. But Banka had no inclination to enjoy their pathetic helplessness. His entire body was shaking in anger. He had imagined that he would cross the threshold of the haunted house and enjoy the beauty of the girl's smile and savour the poison of the vanishing frock. But look at the turn of events, Banka was forced to return home long before evening set in.

Mother asked, "What, the game finished so early today?"

"I have to study more from now on. If I play more I feel drowsy during study hours. I have to stand first in the class during annual examination too," Banka said.

Mother was overwhelmed with joy. "O Bajrangbali, keep on passing such wisdom to my son!" she embraced Banka and planted a kiss on his head.

Mother's kiss filled Banka with disgust. He was already contrite for having deceived his simple mother. He went into the house, picked up a book and tried to read, but he couldn't concentrate on his studies. He should have felt bitter with what had transpired between him and Faka that afternoon, but strangely he felt a deep sense of gratitude towards him. He kept repeating to himself what Faka had told him, like the mantras of the Hanuman Chalisa, the long forty-stanza prayer to the simian god

Hanuman. The more he spoke that line to himself the more he felt the thrill of a pleasurable sensation. He fell into a sleep under the spell of that thrill. As always, after finishing the cooking, Mother woke him up and fed him supper.

Days rolled by. Along came another Sunday, a scorcher really. Sati's mother, with a basket full of stories from all over the universe, turned up at their place to enjoy the weekly camaraderie with her employer. Mother's freedom-loving spirit, oppressed by the demands and responsibilities of the household, sought the benign company of a person her age. She took a break from her sombre and humdrum life in order to indulge in the innocent pleasure of back-biting, fibbing and cribbing about others. As usual, Nani was excluded from the circle. And, as usual, Banka broke into the charmed circle and devoured all their whisperings despite the racket caused by the table-fan running at full speed.

"The belly of the eldest has swollen so big, Sati has seen it at close quarters," Sati's mother was telling her, keeping her tone as low as possible.

"Who, Sonali?" Mother asked.

"I don't know whether it is Sonali or Monali. All three of them are sex-starved bitches. They fight among themselves, always in their hurry to hook a man."

"You can't always blame the girls. When the mother herself invites all kinds of rascals into her house as godsons, what do you expect? It is like nurturing vipers." Mother, who always felt belittled by Mrs. Satpathy's show of physical beauty and wealth, poured out her usual scorn on the mother of the girls.

Banka was unable to understand the link between Mother's anger and the swollen belly of Sonali didi. But he could sense that it was a dangerous situation and rogues like Chheta Singh and Godhi were responsible for it.

"The foolish woman tried to placate these rascals in order to drag her own husband away from the lure of the haunted house, but they in their turn stripped her house of all dignity. Now the entire family plans to shift to her brother's village."

"But the police babu cannot go, leaving his job. Does he plan to stay alone?" Mother asked.

"What other option does he have? He used to visit the haunted house off and on. But the way Mrs. Satpathy tortured that family, they left the place yesterday. It is not practical for the police babu to keep guard day and night." Sati's mother informed.

A strange thudding began in Banka's chest. As if the threshing horse was beating inside him again. His body was drenched with sweat despite the table-fan spinning at full speed. For some reason he felt like crying aloud. He had planned to go to the playground with his bat once the sun started setting. He would practise with Faka, Makara and others. The match with neighbouring sahi was drawing nearer. But now everything seemed detestable to him. The revenge victory in cricket match, placing first in the examination, acing his studies, chocolates from Sonali didi, Mother's kiss, Faka, the shopkeeper's son; all was anathema to him. He had even started hating Bajrangbali, his anchor in all crisis situations.

Banka suddenly got up from his sleeping mat and gulped down a glass of water. His body was shaking uncontrollably. He had not realised that teardrops were rolling down his face. Maybe due to his hurried drinking of water he felt like vomiting, and he rushed out. As soon as he reached the drain crossing the veranda, he began to throw up the water he had drunk.

Mother got up from where she was sitting on the veranda. "What happened? Why are you crying?" Then she placed her palm on his forehead and exclaimed, "My darling, you are running a high fever. Your forehead is almost burning. When did you get this fever? You went to bed after lunch."

She took him to the bedroom and said, "Go sleep on the bed. How many times have I asked you not to drink water after the games? But do you ever listen? From today there is a full stop to all your games."

Then she asked Sati's mother, "Fetch a bowl of cold water and a piece of clean cloth. When the fever subsides we will take him to Dr Giri."

When Banka heard the name of Dr Giri, the fear of an injection left him completely immobile. Mother was applying the soaked piece of cotton to his forehead, sitting beside him on the bed. Sati's mother was gently massaging his hands and legs. He was feeling some comfort no doubt, but he felt consumed inside by a bitter agony and anger.

At some point Mother asked, "Will you still send Sati to do their household chores?"

"God forbid. No, not at all. When Mrs. Satpathy is not around Sati will never cross their threshold. Let the police babu hire some other housemaid. His house may turn into a haunted house for all I care. We are poor people. What else do we have except our honour, dear mother of Banka?"

Banka now realised why mother had asked him not to cross the threshold. All his anger was now concentrated upon Satpathy uncle and the likes of Chheta and Godhi. These people were turning this world into a haunted house. He felt that though he was lying motionless near his mother on the bed, a part of him, having frantically escaped from inside him, was at that very moment crossing the threshold of the house and swimming away towards that evanescent smile and the poison of that receding frock, heedless of any obstacle.

# ALONE

*Translated from "Eka"*

"Last week grandfather had an attack of coronary thrombosis. Now he is under the treatment of J.P. Das," said Satish.

"My father has also been under the treatment of J.P. Das, for the last four years. He is suffering from Pulmonary Stenosis. At regular intervals he has to see the doctor. No, no, not at the Government Medical College Hospital, but in JP's private clinic. Oh my God! Each visit to his clinic costs at least two hundred rupees. Fortunately, my father is a central government employee. His medical expenses are reimbursable. Otherwise how could we afford four to five hundred rupees every month?" came Abinash's rejoinder.

Abinash's story about his family being not well off sounded made-up to Banka. Satish and Abinash were the most affluent students of their class. Satish's father happened to be a wholeseller while Abinash's father served as a high ranking official in the Aviation Research Centre nearby. Most of the students of the school came on foot, but they travelled in their family cars. Spending four to five hundred rupees per month as doctor's fee was child's play for them. By cooking up a story about his family's not so bright finances, Abinash was trying precisely to signal otherwise.

As Banka was contemplating a fitting rebuttal to their tall talk, Kishore Sir entered the classroom. Kishore Sir alias Honourable Guruji Fuji. Banka never could fathom why the students had bestowed such a nickname upon Kishore Sir. But he never referred to him by such a funny name. He always had such great respect for him, for his wide erudition. He liked other teachers too but Kishore Sir's dramatic way of teaching in the class impressed him the most. Unlike others, he never confined himself within the boundaries of curriculum and prescribed texts. He was assigned to teach History, but he could regale the students with delightful anecdotes from all the branches of knowledge including Science, Politics, and Cinema, which were, as it were, on his fingertips. He had the rare ability to fuse the essence of all branches of knowledge with facts of History in such a manner that you started feeling he was not teaching a particular subject but educating you in the intricate art of living.

"Friends," Kishore Sir began in his usual style.

He always addressed students as friends, not by their proper names, even when he met someone alone.

"The knowledge of the subjects you are learning now may have validity within a limited time-frame, till you get a job and get married."

The reference to marriage triggered titters among the girls in the front benches, particularly Sarmistha and Nibedita. Without paying any attention to them Kishore Sir continued, "After marriage, the knowledge you will need on a daily basis is the knowledge of history. The mistakes of history get repeated because we keep on ignoring its lessons. For that reason, and maybe out of exasperation, the great German philosopher Hegel had once remarked, 'The only lesson we learn from history is that we do not learn anything from history.'"

Just then the school peon placed a bunch of answer-sheets on the teacher's table. Murmurs of a subdued excitement spread among the students. The semester examination had ended only a couple of days ago. Nobody thought Kishore Sir would announce the result so soon after checking the answer-sheets. The excitement of the students to find out who had scored how much in History was growing. Without prolonging the atmosphere of excited suspense, Kishore Sir announced, "As usual Bankanidhi Harichandan has scored the highest marks in History, seventy-two." A sense of relief and joy spread through the inner reaches of Banka's mind. "But," Kishore Sir took a long, dramatic pause after uttering that word. Banka felt his chest palpitating. Now a sense of apprehension seized him. His classmates had started looking at him from the corner of their eyes. A sense of shame had already replaced the feeling of joy he had just experienced. "But, being a student of history, I could not ignore its lessons." The honourable Guruji Fuji was trying to thicken the suspense like the plots of detective novels Banka was so fond of reading on the sly during study hours when Mother was not watching. Banka's patience was at the end of its tether. For the first time in his life Banka cursed Kishore Sir silently. He felt there was a grain of truth in what the students said about Guruji Fuji. That he was a braggart and a prattler.

"Many years ago, in my M.A. end-semester examination I managed to score forty-eight marks in my optional paper, European History. Normally, students score more marks in the optional papers than in their core papers. I had also done very well in my optional paper. When I met the professor and Head of the Department regarding such a low score, he was kind enough to fish out my answer-sheet from the stack in his almirah. Spreading it in front of me he explained, 'I had awarded sixty-eight marks to you initially. But then I subtracted twenty marks later because at ten places you have spelt Napoleon wrongly as Nepoleon. The history of modern Europe begins with Napoleon. In my humble opinion one who cannot spell Napoleon correctly does not know a thing about European history. Since you have been a disciplined student I have awarded you forty-eight marks overlooking your gross howler.' Because of my teacher's humble opinion, I was deprived of the minimum qualification to be eligible for a college professor's position. I am preparing you now lest any of my students should suffer a similar fate in future. Bankanidhi misspelt Kaniska as Kanisha at four places in his answer sheet. So, I have deducted eight marks and awarded him sixty-four."

After giving this short speech Kishore Sir reeled out the marks of other students one by one. Banka was not hurt as much by the reduction of his marks as he was perturbed by the fact that Prithiviraj was ahead of him with sixty-six marks. On one hand, Prithiviraj was smart and handsome and, on the other hand, he was way ahead of him in all other matters including debate competition, sport and overall leadership qualities. He always teased Banka with epithets like "studious, the great", "bookworm", "rustic", "bookish fool", just because Banka scored high marks. But Banka knew he was able to get the better of Prithiviraj because of his superiority in studies. Now the fellow's pride would know no bounds for having scored the highest marks in History. His teasing would become more and more acerbic. Inside, Banka's spirit had turned ashen but he projected a calm exterior bereft of any trace of anxiety or loss of face whatsoever.

But after the school hours he could not rein in his emotions. On the way back home his heart was besieged by waves of grief. He could not weep openly on the street lest someone should notice, but kept on rubbing his eyes with a kerchief he took out from his satchel.

"Why are you weeping?" asked Nani who accompanied him.

"No, why should I weep? I got something in my eye and there is itching and burning." Banka explained, although he knew well that it was difficult to evade Nani's eagle-eye easily.

"Where? Let me see." Nani tried to pull the kerchief away from his hand.

"Hey, leave me alone," Banka snapped as he yanked his hand away and ran ahead of Nani. By then they were close to home. Banka kept up the momentum and entered the house at a run. He got rid of the satchel and rinsed his eyes and face thoroughly with water from a bucket.

"Why are you puffing and panting like that?" asked Mother.

"No, nothing," Banka answered. Nani entered the house at that point and declared, "He was rubbing his eyes all the way from school. When I offered to have a look, he ran away."

"Oh my God, his eyes have turned red like a China rose. What can one do with such a child? Hey, why are your eyes swollen like this? What have you done with your eyes?"

Mother worried too much over every trifling thing. Knowing full well that she would not get any satisfactory answers to her questions, she kept haranguing him in a raised voice. Then turning towards Uncle after a while she said, "Take him to the doctor at once. He seems to have hurt his eyes somehow. Oh God! I should rather have died than gone through such a mess?"

Chacha, who spent most of his time relaxing on his bed, came out of his room reluctantly, the signs of irritation, for having his siesta disturbed, writ large on his face. Banka anticipated a fresh round of chastisement from him. But without uttering a single word he coolly escorted him to the clinic of Doctor Mohanty, the eye doctor. A medical representative was detailing the literature of a new product of their company to the doctor when they arrived. On a nearby bench an old bearded rustic, with a turban on his head, was sitting with his eyes closed. An old woman, probably his wife, sat beside him placing her palm on her husband's shoulder. Seeing Banka's swollen red eyes, the old woman addressed Chacha "Son, the child's eyes seem to be red. Why don't you put a few drops of mother's milk on those eyes?"

Just then the medical representative left after bidding good bye to the doctor. When the old woman's patronising words fell on his ears, Doctor Mohanty barked, "Why only mother's milk, if he could add some grains of rice and sugar, one can make a dish of porridge in the eye. O kind hearted aunt, why don't you mind your own business? Leave the treatment of disease to me."

It is true, Banka did not like the doctor's rudeness, but he was amused by the idea of cooking porridge in the eye. Examining his eye under the bright light of a pencil-torch Doctor Mohanty said, "This is viral Keratosis. Take this ointment and apply it before going to bed at night and immediately after he wakes up in the morning. There will be irritation if he goes under the glare of sunlight. Make him wear dark glasses if he has to go outdoors during daytime."

Doctor Mohanty accepted his usual fee only, not the price for the ointment. "This is a sample medicine, not for sale," he explained. On the way back from the clinic Chacha bought him a pair of cheap sunglasses. Banka was eager to put on the dark glasses at once. But it was already late in the night. If he wore the goggles, Uncle would pull him up for being uncouth, rustic. But it was true the glasses looked good in the mirror at the shop while he was trying them on. He fancied he looked like Dev Anand, the movie star, with those glasses on. He silently and heartily thanked those viruses, those Keratosis, meratosis or whatever they were called, for infecting his eyes. For their grace he had this good fortune of owning a pair of goggles for the first time in his life. What if he was unable to wear them during the night? In the morning, when he would go to school wearing those goggles, even the beautiful front-bench girls Sarmistha and Nibedita would be stumped, not to speak of Prithiviraj, his arch rival.

Banka somehow managed to get through the night. The irritation and the burning in his eyes had increased manifold as he woke up in the morning. The pupils looked redder. But Banka was unfazed. After attending to his daily morning chores, he had a quick meal and set out for school much ahead of Nani, wearing the pair of new goggles. On normal days it was Nani who had to coax him to get ready for school.

Noticing his newfound punctuality Nani remarked, "In such a hurry for school? What is the reason Banka?"

"The marks of the English paper will be announced," he shot the answer at Nani and stepped on to the street.

After reaching school, he headed straight towards the ice-cream vendor where Satish and Abinash were enjoying their ice-cream.

A little surprised at Banka's dark glasses, Abinash asked "Want an ice-cream?"

Lacing his tone with some artificial pathos, Banka answered, "No, thank you, brother, I am suffering from viral Keratosis. Don't you see my goggles? If I do not wear them, I might turn blind. Doctor Mohanty warned me last evening."

When Banka was enjoying some self-satisfaction for having given a fitting reply to Satish and Abinash who were boasting yesterday about the sophisticated diseases that ailed their father and grandfather, Hari-pado, their eldest and most weird classmate, suddenly yanked off the goggles and shouted, "Arrey, this fellow has got 'Jai Bangla'. And he is saying viral Keratosis. Don't touch him. It is highly contagious. Go, get away, don't come anywhere near us."

As he shouted, he hurled the goggles into the distance and washed his hands, collecting water from the ice-cream vendor. Fortunately, the goggles were made of cheap plastic, so they did not break. Banka quickly picked up the goggles and wiped the dust off with his kerchief and put them on again. But before he could go back to Satish and Abinash, they had hurried away. Banka was unsuccessful in his objective of winning a psychological victory over them by having an in-depth discussion about his own sophisticated disease. In impotent anger he silently promised revenge on them and spoke to himself, "Wait for my turn, Hari-pado, and just wait for my day. Let me see how you copy answers from my script at the upcoming annual examination. If you ask even once for any answer during the examination, I will immediately complain to the teachers."

Hari-pado was not someone who would be satisfied with that much. Leaving Banka behind, he went straight to the games teacher and petitioned against Banka. "Sir, he is infected with Jai Bangla, but still he has turned up at school. He will infect the rest of the school with this disease."

The newspapers were already rife with frenzied reporting on "Jai Bangla" by that time. More rumours than facts were being dished out. Most of the rumours involved Pakistan. That after getting defeated in the war of 1971, Pakistan had planted a bunch of Bangladeshis in Indian territory. Those Bangladeshis had a dangerous eye infection. Carried by wind those viruses were travelling from eye to eye. This was resulting in deadly Conjunctivitis. Eyes were getting swollen, turning red and in a couple of days healthy human beings were rendered blind. Pakistan's evil design was to turn all Indians blind in this process. When the entire country would be blind, there would be no one left to resist Pakistan's advance into Delhi. Then Pakistan would rule the roost in Delhi. Once Pakistan would be perched in Delhi, what else would remain? Didn't you see what they did in Bangladesh? Women would be raped. Men would be butchered and enslaved. Didn't you see how many Bangladeshis were shot down? Not just Hindus, even the Muslims belonging to their own religion had to undergo abominable suffering. Those who could, somehow fled into Indian territory in order to save their lives. Some of them were now camped in the Dandakaranya forests and others were settled near Chilika lake. All of them carried the deadly eye disease. Was all this not predicted in Malika, the ancient text by Achyutananda, which predicted all future events? The fearsome age of Kali has arrived. Now the streets would be strewn with corpses. Men would feast on human flesh. The only thing that remained to be seen was when Kalia Thakura, the lord of this universe, would be dragged, bound hand and foot, along the high streets of Puri.

Probably the rumours had affected the games teacher somewhat. After listening to Hari's complaint, he summoned Banka.

"Bankanidhi."

"Sir" Banka responded firmly, his pride hurt.

"Why are you wearing goggles?"

"Sir, I am suffering from viral Keratosis. Doctor Mohanty...." He offered to take off the goggles to prove his point. The games teacher panicked. "No, no you need not take them off. You know this is a highly contagious disease. It is airborne. You should not have come to school."

"Why, Doctor Mohanty did not ...."

Cutting into his explanation, the teacher said, "You

go home and take rest at once. I'll tell the headmaster. Arrange a separate place at home for yourself. Otherwise other members of the family might get the infection."

Banka had to return home. The plan he had of shattering Satish and Abinash's pride by bragging about his own sophisticated ailment was in shambles. But what worried him more were the newly purchased goggles. Though of cheap plastic variety, he had hoped to dazzle the beautiful front-bench girls Sarmistha and Nibedita with those goggles and win their hearts. Now, who would care about them at home? While returning home he assuaged his mind with one consolation that now at least he would not have to go to school. At home he could feast upon the World Literature books which he had collected and stowed away for so long. Now no one would prevent him from reading them.

"What! Why did you come back from school? Did you have a fever or what?" Mother asked. "Come let me see."

"Hey, hey, do not touch me. The games teacher told me that I am suffering from 'Jai Bangla'. It is a dangerous contagious disease. From me it might spread to others. Arrange a separate room for me. Otherwise the entire family will go blind." Banka succeeded in driving panic deep into his mother's heart.

"'Jai Bangla', blindness, what all are you blabbering about? O my God, from where did you catch this dreadful disease? Someone tell me what should I do?"

"You need not do a thing. Just arrange a bed in Chacha's room. Nobody should enter that room. Till I am cured let Uncle use my bed. Do it fast. Games teacher has asked me to take complete bed rest. The matter has reached the ears of the headmaster. He has given me special permission to remain absent from school." He felt proud as he narrated his importance to his mother.

Without trying to divine whether Mother was impressed after learning about his importance in school, Banka entered Father's chamber. A few days ago, Father had confiscated his entire collection of the World Literature series lest he should read them during examination time. Now taking advantage of Father's long tour outside the state, he rescued the books from his almirah and brought them over to Uncle's study. In the meantime, Mother had made a bed for him in Uncle's study. As he arranged his books on the study table, Banka thought to himself, "I have time on my hands. I shall read the entire World Literature series one by one leisurely. Who is there to stop me now?"

Removing his goggles, he lay sprawled on the bed. He did not know when he slipped off into a deep slumber and for how long. Nani's voice interrupted his slumber. In a tone of anxiety Nani announced, "Mother, school was closed after half-time. There is an outbreak of some disease called 'Jai Bangla'. A number of students have stayed away from school."

"Is that so? Then Banka was right. He has also been infected by the same, it seems. He has confined himself in that room. Where or who did he get it from, God knows. I don't know what I should do now. Your father is not around too in these trying times."

"Let him be there in that corner room. Don't let Chhotu go anywhere near him. This fellow had volunteered to accompany the group that was collecting relief for the refugees. He might have contracted it during that trip. I tried to prevent him from that jaunt, but he fancies himself to be some Gandhi or Gopabandhu. He just hurried off with the group. Now, who will come to his rescue? If he goes blind then he will realise."

"Oh no! One should not utter those evil words. Keep the ointment on his window sill by the bed so that he can apply it from time to time." Mother instructed Nani.

Banka was sore at Nani's words but as time went by his anger turned into pity for her. She placed his food, water and medicine at regular intervals near his doorstep and cleaned his used utensils. Banka felt proud of this royal treatment. A whole room to himself, food and drinks at proper time, rest to one's heart's content and a heap of delightful books. What else does one need? But when Banka tried to read one of the books after switching on the lights, the letters appeared blurry, and his eyes itched badly. He shut the book and rummaged through Uncle's bookshelf aimlessly.

"Oh my God, what indecent pictures!" The vulgar description that accompanied those pictures triggered dizziness in Banka. His hands, nay, his entire body trembled. His chest started heaving violently. He forgot the itching and burning sensation he had felt a while ago. With his trembling, feverish hands he turned page after page even as he stood motionless near the table. The bevy of dirty pictures and the dirty writing that accompanied them seemed unending. He realised that he should close the book and return to his bed. But there was no energy left in his hands and feet to do that. Fortunately, he heard Uncle's bicycle near the front door. He quickly replaced the book on the shelf and returned to his bed.

"Come to think of it," Chacha was addressing Mother loudly, "this Conjunctivitis seems to have spread widely. Has Banka not contracted this 'Jai Bangla'? I went to Dr Mohanty's clinic to verify. The clinic is closed. Some reported that there were so many patients that the doctor was forced to close the clinic. Others said that Dr Mohanty himself is suffering from 'Jai Bangla'. If the doctor is not able to protect himself, how can he save the patients?"

"Truly! His teacher turned Banka away from school. He has shut himself in the corner room over there. Lest it should spread to others. He might be a bit naughty, but he is conscientious," Mother said.

"He is stayng in that room alone. Will he not be scared at night?" asked Nani.

"He is a grown boy now. What is there to be afraid of inside the house?" Chacha said loudly for Banka to hear, maybe to augment his courage.

Banka had by then switched off the lights in his room for fear of getting caught red-handed. Nani was right. He had already started getting scared as the lights were switched off. But once Uncle had bestowed upon him the honorific of a grown-up boy he had no way of escaping from that lonely room. Who knows how many nights he would have to sleep alone like this in darkness? To ward off the fear of ghosts from his mind he started chanting the Hanuman Chalisa to himself. Before starting the chant he begged forgiveness from the arch celibate Lord Hanuman who might have been angered by his recent act of poring over the red hot stuff from Chacha's bookshelf.

"O Lord Hanuman, Bajrangbali—the one whose body is as firm as divine thunder—I now understand why Uncle is failing in his B.A. examination again and again. But don't thou fail me ever. Let me come first in all examinations. I shall be a teacher like Shankar Sir. If I don't become a teacher, why should Nibedita, the most beautiful girl of the class, marry me? I promise today I will never again look at those books with naked, vulgar pictures or read those provocative descriptions."

The fear of ghosts, of course, was erased from his mind when he remembered Nibedita. A fear of a different kind gripped him, however. Was Uncle telling the truth? Has half of the population including the eye doctor contracted this disease? Has he contracted "Jai Bangla", as Nani was saying? Were all those rumours people were spreading about "Jai Bangla" true? Is the world ending with the Age of Kali? Will there be the great deluge after this? Will all the blind people butcher each other to death? Will the Lord arrive in Kalki Avatar, with His twelve-foot sword, and finally slay those who survived the mutual extermination?

Banka was thoroughly confused. The more he attempted to discipline his mind in order to recite the

Hanuman Chalisa, the more his mind got assailed by these stray thoughts, causing it to swerve away from Lord Hanuman. "Bloody bunch of lecherous sinners." Banka's anger shifted onto the Pakistanis. Why have you set out to loot the honour of other women while you have wives and children at home? Just because you are armed with rifles, you will kill innocent people, appropriate their wealth, rape their women? And all your weapons you will import from China, America? America and China are also strange. They can't sit quietly at home. They will keep themselves safe but at the same time they will incite others to fight among themselves. Is this woman, this arrogant prime minister, any less? She is being provoked by Russia to interfere with the neighbouring country. How is it our business what other countries do, anyway? These refugees came only when we meddled in their matters. Everyone has become blind, clutching their individual egos. Some have grown blind by their own arrogance, some others have been blinded by lust; yet a few others have been blinded by the wealth they plan to earn by selling weapons to others. Kishore Sir was right. We do not learn anything from history. What the blind rulers of the past did, sending their subjects to death to settle their feuds, the so-called political leaders are doing now. These leaders brought in the Bangladeshi refugees. Now many innocent children like Banka will be rendered blind without any fault of theirs.

Will Banka really go blind? The moment this thought entered his mind his fear turned into paralysing terror.

What time of the night was it? Everyone else was in deep slumber by then. He was unable to get any sleep because he had had a long nap during the day. Added to that was this terror of going blind. His chest had begun thumping wildly. He frequently prayed to Hanuman and other sundry gods and goddesses that he could remember. The more frequently he prayed, the greater became his terror. How could he study well if he turned blind? How could he come first in the examinations! If he did not stand first, how could he get a job like Shankar Sir? Would he not fail again and again in his examination like Chacha? What would compel Nibedita to marry a blind boy who repeatedly flunked his examination? He could not think further. Terror and sorrow had choked his throat. Abandoning Hanuman and all the gods and goddesses he felt like hollering to Mother and Nani. But he realised that despite all his efforts no sound came out of his mouth. His hands and feet seemed to have become frozen in acute fright. His body felt transfixed. The only movement was that of the thudding of the heart inside his chest. For a few moments his heart began to race and then slowed down on its own. A little later it started racing again. Who knows how long this see-saw of the heart went on?

When he awoke, it was a couple of hours into the morning, and Nani's voice was at the door. "Banka, Ainthu has come to visit you." Banka got up from the bed with alacrity. His family members like Mother, Uncle and Nani dared not visit him while Ainthu had mustered enough courage to come. He was filled with gratitude for Ainthu. He felt as if Ainthu had given him a new lease on life. Had he not come, the terrible weight of this life of isolation might have turned him mad by now.

Banka enthusiastically welcomed Ainthu who came pushing through the door.

"Come, come. Come right in. Please sit down on the bed. I am probably suffering from 'Jai Bangla' or something. Were you not scared?"

His voice was laced with self-reproach. His earlier euphoria about the happy aftermath of the disease was gone.

Ainthu smiled silently. There were deep and not-so-deep scars left by smallpox on his pitch-dark face. Two rows of shining symmetrical teeth were almost taunting the ghastly unevenness of his face. Far from adding to his beauty the smile actually accentuated his ugliness. Fortunately, Ainthu would never be able to see the horror of his own smiling face. His parents had appropriately named him "Ainthu", the one who had been a leftover of the food of Yama, the lord of Death, Banka thought to himself.

"Your Nani also asked me the same question," said Ainthu. "I said I do not have eyes. Why should I be afraid of 'Jai Bangla' or Jai Anything?"

Strange such a simple thing had not occurred to Banka.

In his early childhood Ainthu had lost both eyes to smallpox. Many parents residing in villages were not aware of vaccines against smallpox in those days.

"Look, Ainthu, now we are in the same boat. What you lost during your early childhood, I am going to lose in my grown-up years. What smallpox did to you, this 'Jai Bangla' is going to do to me."

Banka now felt a new sense of connection with Ainthu. At school no one befriended Ainthu; they spurned his attempts at friendship. That is the reason why Banka took pity on him and went out of his way to chat with him sometimes and share his feelings. But today he felt it was not he who was pitying Ainthu; rather he was a recipient of Ainthu's benediction. How time reversed roles!

"It is some minor eye disease and will heal soon, why are you worrying over it so much? Moreover, is history going to end with smallpox or 'Jai Bangla'? So many things will come and take away much more. Those who cling to things will feel they have lost something. Those who have nothing to lose, how could they be affected? Do you know my grandma always said one thing when I was a child? 'This Ainthu is a blessed soul. Sin will not touch him. Ninety-nine percent of our sins are committed by this accursed pair of eyes.' Of course, I do not know what sins people commit with their eyes."

Banka was immediately reminded of the dirty pictures and descriptions in the books on Chacha's shelf which he had spied upon last evening. The illiterate old woman might have said as much to assuage the feelings of her blind grandson. But the statement was imbued with wisdom and experience! Silently Banka paid obeisance to Ainthu's grandmother. How true was her statement!

Since he had eyes, he was so desperate to marry Nibedita, the most beautiful girl of his class. He needed a good job so that he could marry her. One needed to study well to get a good job. One had to come first in the class. Thinking that these things will not materialise if he went blind, he had spent the entire night in deep terror. This living torment was the meaning of hell. Was there any separate place called hell? Look how Ainthu was sitting with a bewitching smile on his calm visage. He did not even have the ability to find out who was more beautiful, Nibedita or a she-buffalo. He also did not know how hideous he looked when he smiled. Someone else wrote his answers in examinations because he could not write himself. Look how happy and contented he was. Moreover, he had come over to share a part of his happiness with Banka when his own people at home were afraid to come near him.

"Is Ainthu really disabled or is he quite able?" Banka asked himself. Now he was feeling assured because Ainthu was sitting beside him, but the kind of terror he had felt last night in his body, mind and soul made him feel that he had only the illusion of ability. Those so-called abilities might evaporate in a second. It could be due to smallpox in the past, "Jai Bangla" today or something else in the future. When great heroes like Dr Mohanty were hiding in their homes, deserting the battlefield, how puny was his strength! If he went blind due to "Jai Bangla", he would fail miserably in the examination. Let alone the job of a teacher, he might not even secure a lowly position of a peon in some office. Even if he got well, what was the guarantee that he would become a teacher? Some future events like brotherhood between India and China or a strike of the Sputnik or the fall of some residue of an Apollo spacecraft could kill him. His entire future might be blighted by any such catastrophe. Maybe he would survive and make it, but Nibedita, the queen of his heart, might vanish without a trace. It was all a play of uncertainty. Amidst this entire uncertainty one could be free of terror like Ainthu only if one were able to get rid of all kinds of illusions. That, in fact, would be bliss.

"Ainthu my brother, it is not that you have lost your eyes, you have been released from the trap of illusion. You really are a man of beatific vision though you do not possess physical eyes."

"Why did you say this?" Ainthu asked innocently.

"No, nothing serious. You should visit me now and then. I feel really good." Banka tried to change the subject.

"I will come every morning till you get well. I heard that they are going to close the school long before the Christmas holidays. For this 'Jai Bangla' outbreak."

"And if I go blind then we will be sinless and pure souls together," Banka said in a chatty vein.

The two friends laughed. This time around Ainthu's laughter did not look hideous to Banka's diseased eyes.

# RESOLUTION

*Translated from "Sankalpa"*

The bell tinkled as soon as evening set in. After offering a lighted wick at the holy basil plant, Mother was at her aarti in the prayer room. Tying one end of her saree around her neck she rotated one hand that held the burning lamp before the gods, lighting up their visages, while with the other hand she rang the bell continuously. An enclosure in one corner of the back veranda passed for the prayer room. In it small statues and framed photographs of various gods and goddesses were arranged upon a huge stand made from the wood of a mango tree. Every morning and evening Mother would rotate a lamp before the deities, ring the bell, light incense sticks and blow the conch-shell. Then she would go to the kitchen across the courtyard. The prayer room was clearly visible from the veranda of the kitchen allowing Mother to keep watch on the activities of the children. In the evening all the children had to sit in front of the statues of the gods and pray. Then they would sit down to study. Banka would pray too, but more out of fear for his mother.

They were to recite the prayer loudly, loud enough to be audible to Mother:

"O Compassionate Lord, the wanderer of the Universe." It was initially very awkward for Banka to recite the prayer so loudly. The prayer was the signal for the grandmother in the neighbouring house to sound an alert to her grandchildren:

"The jackals have started howling. It is already dark. Come back home now."

What a shame! Was God hard of hearing that one had to pray so loudly? Why did his grandmother not pray so loudly when she visited them? She seemed to be the most devout in the family. She spent the morning hours inside the prayer room. Maybe she wanted to avoid the household chores. Who knows? Her small white bag would be stuffed with holy basil beads. Her fingers would be inside the bag shuffling those beads, whimpering because of stomach pain. She would wait for everyone to finish eating their breakfast. When it was time for her own breakfast to be served she would reluctantly approach her food. She never prayed volubly. Once a week, on Sundays, Father went into the prayer-room, but never prayed loudly. Lighting a lamp, he read the Gita silently. The chachas never came anywhere near the prayer room. Grandfather counted his beads throughout the day. He would be reading newspapers, listening to the radio as he counted his beads. If somebody asked a question he would answer, his hand still inside his bag of beads. The eldest chacha probably did not believe in gods and goddesses. But he had the most comfortable life. Father rode a bicycle to his office while an office jeep took the eldest chacha to his workplace. A khaki uniform-clad peon carried his office files.

The school was no different. The teachers would stand quietly wearing colourful dresses and sarees. Wearing dull school uniforms, Banka and his school mates would recite the prayer at the top of their voices. Many lady teachers and the headmaster never came near the prayer quadrangle which was very close to the headmaster's office. Apparently, the headmaster was a busy man. It looked as though the busier people were, less was their need for prayer. It was only left to the likes of Banka to pray. If he could land a lucrative job, Banka often thought, he could escape this drudgery of prayer. If prayer was so meaningless, why did Mother force them to pray, that too in a loud voice? Her firm order was that their voices should be audible to her in the kitchen. The entire locality could hear their din. It had even earned them the nickname of a "pack of jackals". They'd became the butt of neighbourhood children's jokes.

"O Compassionate Lord, the wanderer of the Universe," Nani was singing full throttle. Quickly pouring a mug of water on his feet, Banka sat down to pray, his feet still wet. Unwashed feet were ill-omened and Nani would complain to Mother or Chacha.

Nani was a difficult kind of customer. She had a terrible voice which she unleashed without any rhyme or rhythm during prayer, as if her devotion flowed like the urine of a bullock. Since she had no friends and was uninterested in any kind of sports or games, she was very keen on prayer. Moreover, she was always looking for an opportunity to complain about Banka. This was her ploy to endear herself to the elders. Chacha's palms were forever itching to let loose a volley of fists and slaps as soon as the allegation was registered. A box on Banka's ear with his palm that was coarser than a farmhand's made his face boil for an hour as if all the five elements of his being had shattered into smithereens. The less said about the punishment meted out by Mother, the better. She would not punish on a regular basis. But if she decided to vent her anger once in a while she would pull out all the stops. She would pick up whatever came to her hand and start thrashing him, causing welts to appear all over his body. But after a while she would start weeping in remorse, and tend to the wounds with ointment. That day there would be no cooking. Chacha would fetch roti and curry from a nearby eatery. Banka's share of the food would be so small that it would hardly satisfy his hunger. His aching body and hungry stomach would rob him of a good sleep at night.

Did Mother thrash him because she was sick and tired of the endless rounds of household chores? Or because of some tiff with Father or the chachas? Or because of the silent-faced, and conspiratorial Chachi? Whenever Bua Ranu visited them, she would definitely trigger some explosion at home. She would go straight to Grandmother and unveil her list of complaints. Both mother and daughter would then sit together, weeping for a long time. When their weeping would subside Grandmother would take out the best sarees and other valuables from Mother's box and hand them over to his aunt. Bua Ranu would put all these items in her bag. She would be escorted back to her in-laws' place in a rickshaw by Father.

On those days, when Father returned from office, a new drama would unfold at home. Mother would sulk for several days and curse her own bad fate. Father would be unusually quiet and helpless. As it was, Father was indifferent to affairs at home. He never bothered about whether Nani went to school or to which class Banka was promoted. His only passion seemed to be attending to his office work regularly and in time. At home he usually kept himself confined to books or newspapers. His conversations with family members were restricted to monosyllables. But, if for some reason he lost his temper, he was beyond control. There would be a tornado at home. All furniture would be thrown around; the mosquito nets would be torn, glass items would be broken. No one would be spared his fury. Grandmother and Mother would hide in the kitchen. Peace would be restored after three to four hours, after he had spent all his energy. It would take the chachas a couple of hours more to clear the debris and set the house back in order. A long time would elapse before another such tornado took place.

One such tornado happened when Chacha failed

in the matriculation examination for the first time. Unfortunately, it was quickly succeeded by another one due to Banka himself. After Chacha failed, Father had taken some interest in the children's studies. At least on Sundays he started supervising their lessons during study hours.

One Sunday Banka was going through his history textbook. Father asked him, "Who is the father of Akbar?" Startled, Banka answered, "Babar."

Father roared, "Akbar's father's name is Babar? Is this the history you are reading?" The history book fell from Banka's hands at that roar and along with it fell the detective novel of Kanduri Das that was hidden inside it. Now Father's anger had to be seen to be believed. The first slap itself made Banka pee in his pants. The thrashing continued even as he stood immobile with his wet pants. The thrashing that day was so severe that Mother and Grandmother had to intervene, taking some of the beatings on themselves. Father left the place in a huff and went straight to the headmaster. Banka heard later that the headmaster had instructed the History teacher Nanda Sir to pay special attention to Banka.

But Banka had been completely devastated. What was the point of such a life full of abuse and beatings? Was it such a sin, not to know the name of Akbar's father? Was it a crime to read the detective novels of Kanduri Das? Chaga, Danei, Fakira and others read Mastram's book *Night in a Bamboo Grove* inside the classroom, and they watched pornographic sketches. They regularly bought books with yellow covers at the store near the railway station. They never got beaten up like animals the way he was. Faka, of course, had been severely beaten up by a teacher at school on one occasion. But that was because of a grave crime he had committed. He had once clasped Preeti during lunch break. It was rumoured that Banamali Sir was in love with her. When others failed to work out their sums he used to punish them. But he patiently explained the sums to her. She too smiled at him very often. Banka enjoyed her smiles a lot; but she smiled only when Banamali Sir was around. That day, after Faka's misadventure, Banamali Sir was so enraged that he broke three canes on Faka's body. Banka was delighted with the punishment meted out to Faka. But at that same time he was sore with Banamali Sir, too. He was convinced that Sir was also a sinner. He should not have designs on so young a girl as Preeti. But nobody ever punished Banamali Sir for his sins. Instead, it seemed fate had singled Banka out for all the punishments, abuse and thrashings. Why should he continue to live with such a fate?

He decided to take his own life. Instead of going to the playground in the evening he went up to the roof. For a long time nobody had gone to the roof since the banisters had been blown away during the last cyclone. The children were specially prohibited from going to the roof. In the faint light of dusk, Banka could recognise the white spots of pigeon droppings dotting the entire roof. He tiptoed his way towards the edge of the roof, carefully avoiding stepping on the gobs of shit. He stood at the spot where a big chunk of the banister had caved in. While he contemplated jumping, his body turned cold in fear. His head reeled. A nice, cold, winnowing wind wafted across his body as he stood still on the rooftop. It probably was a full-moon night. The moon appeared so large and so close. Should he jump down? How would his mother take his death? And Preeti? Because he was a good student, Preeti sometimes gave him sidelong glances. When he was dead, what would Preeti see when she came by? His entire body, his legs and hands reduced to a mangled lump of flesh, blood splattered all over the road in little pools. The place would resemble the spot near the butcher Babu Mian's meat shop after the goats were slaughtered. His pants would be smeared with his own shit. It was said a person passed stool when he died by suicide. He remembered the dead body of the woman who had hung herself in the house of Sati's mother, how the policemen had flipped and turned the woman's naked body. When he was dead they would also turn his naked body around in front of Preeti! Oh! My god.... He could not think any further.

O Compassionate Lord, the wanderer of the universe

Nani's raucous voice rang out precisely at that moment. Before he could think any further, his habituated feet led him swiftly towards the corner of the veranda designated as the prayer room. Sitting down near Nani and Chhotu, he started in a sing-song voice:

Kindly heed my pleadings.

What should he plead for before god? Should it be "O Lord Bajrangbali, give me enough strength to commit suicide? That nobody should come to see me after my death? Or remove all kinds of anger, abuse and beating from this world"?

But nothing ever happened according to his prayers. Every evening he prayed along with Nani to ignite auspicious thoughts in his mind. His pleas for strength in his body, and courage in his mind seemed to melt into thin air. Ultimately, he had come to believe that either God was not omnipresent or He did not have that thing called kindness. Had his power been manifest everywhere, Father would not be working so hard to feed a bunch of indolent fools. Just because he was forced to work so hard, he was probably venting his anger by thrashing his children. Had God been omnipotent, Chacha would not have failed again and again in his examination. He would also not take his frustration out on Banka by hitting him whenever there was an opportunity. Had God been omniscient, Banka would have been able to remember the names of Akbar's grandfather, great grandfather and great great grandfather, let alone his father. He would not have been hit by Mother with a split piece of wood or a rolling-pin for not being able to memorise his lessons. His visage would have been like that of the film star Rajesh Khanna. Preeti would have fallen in love with him and not with Banamali Sir who was already married and had fathered several children. So what was the point in barking these prayers so loudly? Rather, Faka's life was worth much more. When the prayer was sung at school, Faka used to sing a parody of it:

O Compassionate Lord, the wanderer of the Universe
Accept my pleadings to your heart
Take care of the patch of green in your backyard
And eat it by cutting it.

His limerick goes on and on, parodying the prayer till he reaches his last lines:

Teach me only this O Lord,
Not to want a buxom young lass in my bed.

Banka enjoyed Faka's parody a lot. He also felt like singing similar songs. But he was scared lest the teachers should overhear what he was singing. He was afraid of the punishment that would follow. Moreover, if there was really some omnipresent, omniscient, omnipotent God somewhere and this God somehow heard such a prayer, what might be the nature of the punishment! True, nothing had ever happened to Faka. But who could guarantee nothing would happen to Banka if he too indulged in such blasphemy? So he had decided to be quiet while others prayed at school or at home. Once in a while he lip-synced, just to give the impression that he was praying with all sincerity like the others.

How Banka envied Faka's freedom and daring! He did not have the courage to blaspheme like him. Or to lampoon the teachers, to tease the girls or raid their tiffin-boxes at lunch time. He did not have Faka's strength to bring down opponents in football matches. Nor his tolerance for regular beatings and humiliation at the hands of the teachers. Banka would have loved to enjoy that freedom, that devil-may-care attitude Faka displayed. But the fear of God held him back. But why did he never punish Faka? How come he got promoted in all examinations even though he cheated?

> On earth, forests, sky and water
> Your lila can be felt everywhere.

While Banka was trying to sync his lip movement with Nani's rhythmic voice, the prayer went on even as Chhotu struggled to tag along in his nasal tone.

What divine play, what lila you have spawned, Oh Lord? With these creatures like Faka at the helm? All the courage, all the strength seemed to be with these wretches. All the beauty, all the sophistication was with people like Banamali Sir, who were already married and had sired children. All of them must have sung this prayer in their childhood, "Teach me only this O Lord, I need nothing else, neither men nor money." One was taught to always tell the truth. Then, one was also told to shun riches. Why, then, was everybody running like mad to offices, courts, and other places of work? Why was there so much pressure to study well? Why were people getting married? They were praying one way and acting in another? Were they all telling the truth always, his father, mother, chacha and others? Faka was far better than them. Although he was a rascal, his prayers and his deeds matched. Everybody else was a hypocrite. This prayer was false. So was this the omnipresent, omnipotent and omniscient God? Chacha, Nani, Father, Mother all were liars. Was Mother a liar also? It was not easy to believe that. Might be Mother was not false. Had she been false, why would she cry whenever she beat Banka? Why did she apply balm to his bruises? Then this omnipresent God might be true after all. Now Banka spelt out his final resolution.

"O Omnipresent God, if you are true, then listen to my prayer, carefully. You are supposed to know even the inner thoughts of human beings. So I do not want to make false prayers to you in a loud voice. I am letting you know what all I really want from you. First of all, make me an adult, as soon as possible. Fill my body with a lot of strength. I don't need this strength to serve the poor, the needy and the helpless. I want to beat into a pulp all those who, like Faka, terrorise others. I want to destroy rascals like Faka, Chacha and Banamali Sir, till there is no trace of them. I need enough strength for that. I do not want to live with these honest people like Nani, Chaga and Beena who keep quiet even while they witness the suffering of others at the hands of wicked men. I should have the courage to torture those who do not think twice before hurting me. If you want to provide some positive thoughts, pack them into the minds of these adults, fathers, mothers, grandfathers, grandmothers and chachas. So that they won't beat children mercilessly when the children do not study or refuse to pray. Let no one's dinner be denied him if he fails to remember the name of Akbar's father or grandfather. Let the adults have real trust in your abilities. O Lord, let them have faith in the fact that the entire universe is being run according to your will. Let them not be overly worried because someone could not remember some lesson or did badly in one examination or two. If one is bored of reading textbooks all the time, they should be free to read detective novels of Kanduri Das."

At last, he marshalled all his courage and blurted out the prayer which he had been contemplating for a long time, but had not been able to articulate: "O Lord of the Universe, I need wealth and power over men. Why should I pray falsely that I do not need them? Had I not just prayed a little earlier that I would tell the truth even at the cost of my life? I desperately need wealth and influence over men. I need to become a great man. Otherwise why am I taking all this trouble to study well? If I had wealth and power I would not be afraid of any one. I would not be beaten up by Father and the chachas. I also need four to five voluptuous young girls like Preeti. Only then can I teach a proper lesson to that perverted Banamali Sir."

After he finished his prayer, Banka felt an unusual sensation course through his body. It was different from the numbing sensation he had felt while standing near the banister of the roof, contemplating suicide. This was a joyous sensation that made his entire body glow. Although he was sitting with his eyes closed, he felt a wave of glowing light splashing across his body. Had the Lord really heard his prayer? Banka felt that this wave of joy and light was the result of something having been set free deep inside him. Whether there was any God or not, whether He really heard people's prayers or not, this light and joy was possible because he had found the prayer he had kept bottled up inside him. Was the truth inside him, was the bottled-up prayer also for the Lord, the omnipresent God? Then what about the truth inside Faka, his prayer? Father's anger, Mother's broomstick, Chacha's coarse ear-boxing, Nani's out-of-tune singing...?

The joy and light filling him was starting to ebb away. When he came to himself, he realised that Nani and Chhotu had already left the prayer room after finishing their prayer. Chhotu had started barking A for apple, B for bat from the study room. How long had he been sitting like this with closed eyes? For how long?

"Banka is praying with great devotion today, for a long time." He heard Mother's delighted remark.

"Yes, he will become Vivekananda overnight." Chacha joined in sarcastically. "This is his ploy not to study." Then raising his voice a little, he addressed Banka, "Get up now. We do not need such earnest devotion. Go, work out at least ten sums. I will check in an hour."

Banka felt like blurting out, "What? Will you supervise my mathematics? You have already failed thrice in the matriculation examination. Go take care of your own studies." But, for reasons best known to him, he did not say anything and quietly proceeded towards his books and notebooks.

# TIMETABLE

*Translated from "Routine"*

It was Hari-pado who raised his hand first. Hari had earned the suffix for his tendency towards flatulence. The entire class burst out laughing when Hari raised his hand. Even the girls on the front benches laughed although they tried to smother their laughter with their stoles. Preeti, the most beautiful girl of the class, was bubbling inside with laughter despite her reputation as the most sober and studious girl. No one believed that Hari would be the first student to accomplish the task assigned by the teacher. His image as the oldest boy in the class and as a dunce, not to mention his other peccadilloes, reinforced this sense of disbelief. Naturally, him raising his hand sent ripples of laughter and giggles across the class. But Sankar Sir was standing gravely as usual. Two sets of sparkling white teeth were dazzling from behind his half-opened mouth. Ah! What beautiful symmetry in those two rows of teeth! I will be just like Sankar Sir, when I grow up, Banka thought to himself. I will also be a teacher like him. I will sport such a brilliant thin moustache. I will wear a navy blue shirt on top of a pair of white trousers. I will tuck the shirt inside the trousers and fasten a shining black belt to hold the trousers in their place. Ah! If Preeti only agreed to marry me!

'Sir, Harishchandra.' Banka was transported back from his world of day-dreaming by the grave, booming voice of Sankar Sir. Students had also stopped their squealing by that time.

"So you have already prepared the schedule?" The teacher was asking in his usual serious tone.

Harishchandra Sahu, alias Hari-pado alias Grandpa, alias The King of Meghana bidis stood up and answered, "Yes, Sir."

At that point he had become aware that no one except him had prepared the timetable. His face had acquired a glow of pride by then. He was overjoyed by the fact that for the first time in his life he had accomplished a task assigned by the teacher before anyone else. Especially when even the monitor and the better students of the class had not done so. He was angling for some well-deserved praise from the teacher. He got up from the bench and handed over a large piece of paper with lines drawn on it.

Sankar Sir held the paper and started reading the contents with a great deal of interest. Banka was waiting expectantly for Sankar Sir's reaction. Hari had been advanced to class eleven this year along with Banka and the others after failing once or twice in each of the previous classes. He never bothered about his studies, although otherwise he was a genuinely innocent boy. He was way above everybody in the class in age, but had become the target of collective ridicule. Someone would pull his shirt; a few others would paste chewing gum onto his hair. More ingenious students would draw a picture of an ass on a piece of paper and paste it on his back. Had he so wished he could have beaten a couple of them to pulp, but Hari ended up scolding them in foul language with tears streaming from his eyes. Vulgar language from Hari's mouth sounded like Vedic mantras to some, so they would tease him deliberately only to hear his curses and imprecations. Hari would get some relief only after cursing them in vulgar language to his heart's content, and the boys would enter the class after this bout of cursing from Hari, satisfied with their prank.

After going through Hari's timetable, Sankar Sir burst into a roar of laughter. Banka got scared. Sankar Sir's laughter was not an auspicious sign at all. He had the reputation of being the angriest teacher in the entire school. He was always very trim, both physically as well as in his sartorial choices, taught his class well, but never laughed. On occasions when he laughed, you could well predict that someone was going to have a very bad day. He would start beating that boy mercilessly while he continued to laugh loudly.

"Sriman Harishchandra Sahu," Sankar Sir asked, stopping his laughter abruptly, "When are you going to smoke bidis? There seems to be no time allotted for smoking bidis in your timetable?"

The mention of bidis triggered a collective memory. A few days ago, Hari sat on top of the school wall. Every evening he came to the school playground for an intake of fresh air. That day, for some reason, he sat atop the wall, his legs dangling downwards towards the road on the other side. The school headmaster had been held back in his office that evening over some work. When he headed home after dark he could figure out someone was sitting on the wall smoking a bidi and singing a film song loudly. Since the person was sitting with his back towards him he could not see the face of the person. When he came closer he realised it was Hari.

"Hari, what are you doing?' he shouted.

When Hari heard the voice of the headmaster he nervously jumped on to the ground and blurted out, "Sir, I am smoking a bidi."

Although Hari uttered the words in a panic, his sudden jump startled the headmaster making him fall off his bicycle. Fortunately, the school peon was following the headmaster and he helped the headmaster get up, gather his wits about him, and go home. Hari's skin was saved because of this mishap, otherwise he would have either been expelled from school or received a severe cane-thrashing. The headmaster did not take the matter further. But the deputy headmaster Bhagabat Sir somehow got wind of the incident. He did not get on well with the headmaster at all. So, the story of the incident circulated from ear to ear till the entire school had heard it. It turned into a popular joke. Boys started asking, “So, Hari, when do you smoke bidis?” In all innocence, Hari would answer, “Yes, once or twice while answering nature’s call.” The boys would be in stitches at his response but Hari failed to understand why they were laughing.

Now, the entire class again burst out laughing when Sankar Sir alluded to that incident. Hari was looking around him, completely confused by the commotion. Then Sankar Sir started reading Hari’s timetable aloud. “Mathematics from six o’clock in the morning to eight o’clock. From eight to ten English. School hours from ten to four. In the afternoon, from four o’clock to six o’clock in the evening, General Science. From six to eight, Social Science, from eight to ten, Sanskrit. From ten o’clock to midnight, Literature. From midnight to four o’clock in the morning, Sleep. Get up at four o’clock for morning ablutions. Prayer from five o’clock to six o’clock in the morning. Then again from six o’clock...”

“Bloody hell, Hari, you seem to have surpassed Mahatma Gandhi...!” Sankar Sir’s tone shifted from mock praise to the usual angry one. “Hey, Mukunda, fetch some good, sturdy canes,” he hollered for the school peon. The entire class stopped laughing and was stunned into silence at Sankar Sir’s command.

Hari had reckoned the teacher would be pleased with his prompt accomplishment of the task. For the first time in his life he would have his fair share of praise. But when he heard canes were being ordered, he was terrified.

“Sir, this is not my fault. It was Dama bhai,” he hurried with his answer.

"Who is this bloody Dama bhai?" Sankar Sir nearly yelled.

"My elder brother, Sir."

"What is he?"

"A matric-fail. He was studying in OTM High School. He failed thrice. Father asked him not to study any more. Now he is sitting at home. When I told him Sir has asked me to prepare a timetable, he volunteered to do it for me," Hari explained.

After the pre-test examination Sankar Sir had told them, "Now you will take the matriculation examination. This is the most challenging examination in your life. Your entire career is dependent upon the result of this exam. Your entire future. So, the coming six months will be the most important period of your life. If you idle this time away, you may never blossom in your life. Start studying in a disciplined manner. Divide the entire time of the day between various subjects. Prepare a schedule indicating the time when you should study a particular subject, follow that schedule. Keep Sundays aside for the revision of the subjects already covered. On that day take a self-test with the help of a standard test paper. Check whether you are able to finish answering the questions in the test paper in the time allotted for the final examination. Before going to bed at night make a note in your diary of the topics you could cover and how much you could cover of the task you set yourself for the day. And remember, set more time for Mathematics and English in your timetable."

That day, Sankar Sir's exhortation had been very inspiring for all. It was stirring even for Banka Harichandan who stood first in most exams. He thought to himself that he would also prepare a timetable and apply himself to rigorous studies if he had to secure one of the top ten positions in the State ranking. He would disprove the common perception about him that, though he was a good student, he was rather careless about his studies. But he had not reckoned with Hari turning timetable-making into such a farce.

"Let's rejoice that Harishchandra has been truthful so far," Sankar Sir spoke in a grave tone. "So, Mukunda, take back the canes." He instructed the peon, who was standing in attention, smiling at the students. The students felt reassured. No one wanted Hari caned.

"Look children, there is no guarantee that everyone will excel in studies. But you should never stop trying your best. Whatever may be the work, to do it sincerely is a real human quality. Whether we will excel in our studies may not be in our hands, but to strive to excel is in our hands. So strive for that wholeheartedly. Work so hard that you do not have time to think a bad thought let alone do a bad deed. Now you are all students. It is your task to concentrate on your studies. If Sriman Harishchandra had not spent his time smoking bidis and watching movies, he might not have had the ignominy of failing in exams again and again. But since he has confessed the truth all his past misdeeds are forgiven. Let us expect he will be truthful in the days to come. He will concentrate on his studies and give up his bad habits. He, along with other students of the class, will matriculate and bring glory to the school."

The bell for lunch-break rang as Sankar Sir finished his exhortation. Saturday being a half-day, that was the final bell. Banka headed home at once. The words of Sankar Sir had filled him with great enthusiasm. He would neither be unruly like Hari nor prepare a timetable which would be an object of ridicule. He would draw up a timetable with great care. He would prepare for the tests accordingly. He would build his career. There would have to be a complete full stop to bidi-smoking which he had indulged in a couple of times with Hari during lunch-break, at the fruit orchard of the local government nursery. From now on studies, only studies.

Banka had planned to prepare the timetable at home right after having a snack. But Ashis turned up just then. The captain of their sahi cricket team. On Saturdays when school got over early they usually had a long practice session.

"Aren't you ready? Tomorrow we have a match against Pareswar Sahi," Ashis said.

"My friend, I can't play in the match. My matriculation examination is at hand. I have to start preparing from today. You better take away the kitbag," Banka told Ashis while handing over the kit stored in the attic of the house. He was feeling guilty even while he said this. Ashis also looked troubled.

"You may not play in the match but teach our players

your spin bowling during practice. The spin bowler of our team has joined the famous Madanmohan Cricket Club. If our boys do not practise against good spin bowling they cannot stand up to Amulya's craftiness during the match tomorrow."

Banka was already feeling guilty when he said that he would not play in the match. The thought that the prestige of their sahi would be compromised because of him filled him with sadness. His reputation as a good spin bowler struck terror among other cricket teams. Should he betray his team just before the match? It was not possible for Banka to ignore Ashis's request anymore. He assured him, "Okay, I will bowl ten to fifteen overs and then come back."

Banka forgot the promise he made to himself after reaching the playground. He felt he was bowling far better than on other days. He was taken aback by how the balls released from his hand spun viciously into the stumps from both sides. Forget ten to fifteen overs, Banka went on playing longer than usual, getting carried away by his own skilful performance. It was late in the evening when Banka returned from the playground. He was scared. If for some reason Father had returned home early from office or if Chacha was at home then it would be disastrous. Moreover, if he did not prepare the timetable in the course of the evening his own resolve to begin serious preparations for the ensuing examination would be thwarted.

Fortunately, neither Father nor Chacha had returned

by the time Banka reached home. Grandmother was busy counting the beads. Mother was in the kitchen. Nani, his elder sister, and Chhotu, his younger brother, were just finishing their loud evening prayer which resembled the howl of jackals. After washing his hands and feet Banka bowed down before Bajrangbali's idol in front of the prayer room. Then he went straight to the corner where he studied regularly. He rolled down a mat and sat down with his text and notebooks. Nani was so stunned by his devotion to studies that she forgot to lodge a complaint against him to Mother. On the contrary, when Banka requested it, she passed her long ruler to him without a word.

Banka pulled out a huge piece of paper from the rack and started drawing lines with the help of the ruler. Six straight horizontal lines along the length of the paper. For the seven days of the week. He was so enthused by his own sense of duty and promptness that his mind was free of all ill will. He was feeling a divine affection, unknown to him so far, for everyone. For Nani who endeared herself to Chacha, Father, Grandmother and Mother by constantly reporting his so-called misdeeds; for Chacha who boxed his ears now and then for no reason even as he shuffled around the house like a dandy, clad in a churidar and panjabi (kurta), imitating the attire of film hero Rajesh Khanna in the movie "Hathi Mere Sathi"; for Mother who thrashed him mercilessly if he did not say his prayer in the evenings or did not do well in exams; for Father who forced him to kneel if he played cricket for too long; for Grandmother who indulged in all kinds of evil gossip even as she kept on shuffling the beads throughout the day; for Grandfather who forcibly woke him early in the morning and barked a bunch of unintelligible Sanskrit shlokas into his ears; for Bhagabat Sir who was unduly soft towards Preeti, the prettiest girl in his class. Sankar Sir was right after all. This feeling of affection is the sign of a good human being. The moment he decided to be dutiful, to study attentively, everyone, nay the entire creation, appeared friendly to him.

Now, with renewed enthusiasm, Banka set out to draw vertical lines on the paper. One, two, three. How many periods during the morning hours? At best he can have three hours. From six o'clock in the morning to nine o'clock. Then one has to take a bath, have one's meal and reach school by ten o'clock. One needs to cover eight subjects during three hours. There was an alternative, though. One could study three subjects in the morning and the remaining five in the evening. If he gave up playing in the afternoon for the next six months, then he could squeeze in five hours of studies in the evening. Should one devote one hour to each subject? Sankar Sir had said to devote more time to Mathematics and English. Let us then earmark an hour and a half each for Maths and English in the mornings. Then if one devoted forty-five minutes to each subject, it would take four and a half hours to cover all subjects.

But can one do justice to one subject in forty-five minutes? What if one studied a subject once in two days?

Would one not forget a subject if one did not study it daily? Should one mention the school timings in the routine? Is it worth mentioning in the routine the timings for brushing the teeth, going to the toilet, mealtimes, the evening prayer, short walks to keep one's mind fresh? During these short walks he had the habit of thinking of Preeti. During those moments Preeti's blushing face flashed so often in his mind, his bones would burn in anger when he remembered the way Bhagabat Sir pressed her cheek in mock-anger. Even in the playground if he remembered the scene he became so disoriented that he bowled his deliveries without any line or length. If Kama bhai was batting on the other side it would be the end of the matter. He would tear into his bowling, hitting a flurry of sixes till Banka got his form back.

If he completely gave up playing games could he set aside a time in his routine for thinking about Preeti? Oh God, what a shame it would be! Moreover, leave aside Sankar Sir, if Father came to know of this he would beat him like Mother beat ginger to a pulp while cooking. Banka felt sad when he remembered Father's brutal beatings. When he felt sad or wanted to escape beatings he often prayed to Bajrangbali. Should he also mention prayer in the routine? But nobody knew that he prayed to Bajrangbali and at times scolded him. If they came to know of this they would mock him. Maybe they would also come to know that he had once promised to offer a bunch of bananas if he stood first in the examination. As wished, he actually came first in the class. Once the results were out he took some money from Mother and offered a bunch of ripe bananas to the deity. Strangely, after the offering, the overripe bananas seemed to become raw and tasted astringent like raw bananas. Banka told himself that Bajrangbali had invisibly sucked all the sweetness from those bananas. When he became sure of this he ate those astringent bananas with great relish, although he did not reveal this to anyone.

Would it not be easier to offer more bananas to Bajrangbali than getting into this hassle of preparing a schedule to be successful in the examination? He could also offer a bunch of bananas every day for a month before the examination. He could then pray to be included in the list of top ten students. Mother would not mind spending money on these offerings. Otherwise he could steal some money from Grandfather's purse. If that could be arranged he might be able to play in tomorrow's cricket match. He could capture wicket after wicket and leave the Pareswar Sahi team in shambles. He could return from the playground on the shoulders of his teammates as the man-of-the match. He would be so happy that he would not feel any hunger or thirst for a week. The only regret was, although the matches were played in the school playground, Preeti never came to watch any of them.

Wouldn't Bajrangbali be angry if he filched money from Grandfather's purse? And won't his big career plans come crashing down if the simian god was displeased? He had to become a teacher like Sankar Sir, wear a shirt, trousers and belt like him. He had to teach in the classroom. To become like him he did not only have to pass matriculation but several more examinations in college. Would he have to offer bananas before each examination? What if after becoming a teacher, he did not know how to teach in the class? Would he not suffer the plight of the Physical Education teacher of the school who was sent as a substitute if the regular teacher was on leave? How happy the students are when the PET came! The naughty students asked him to solve the most difficult sums or to explain the most complex English passages or poem in the text. The person who, with a whistle in the mouth, had hundreds of students under his thumb in the playground, looked pathetic inside the classroom. To cover up his helplessness he would suggest, "let's have a song competition." The students echoed in a chorus, "Boys on one side and girls on the other." Banka would wait for Preeti to sing a song to which he could respond. But bashful Preeti never sang. Banka waited in vain. Although those classes appeared delightful to others, Banka felt a strange despondence. He would get angry with Preeti and feel pity for the PET. If after becoming a teacher he does not know how to teach, the students might pity him. While teaching in the class he can neither pray to Bajrangbali nor placate the god with offerings.

"Hey Banka, are you studying or dozing?" Banka was startled by Chacha's voice. "Go fetch four paans from Kalu's shop for me."

"You came back only ten minutes ago. You could not fetch paan yourself and now you are sending him," Mother shouted back at Chacha from the kitchen. "Looks like the mood is on him, as he has been studying since early evening. Do not disturb him now."

"Dear sister-in-law, come and see what your darling son is doing since early evening." Chacha shouted back from Banka's study corner.

"I am preparing a timetable. Sankar Sir has asked us to make it and show it to him first and then prepare for the examination accordingly," Banka explained, pointing at the stack of paper, pencil, scale and eraser in front of him.

"Good, good. Keep dozing in the name of preparing the timetable. You rogue, every year you prepare hundred such schedules. But when do you study? What value is there in a mere timetable however well-made it is?" Chacha's harsh words kept on piling thick and fast.

It was true. Banka remembered when he appeared at the scholarship examination. He also remembered each annual examination. Before each examination he prepared such timetables. Nobody knew about it, but he never abided by the regimen he prescribed for himself. Does Chacha ever abide by any discipline? Had he done so, he would not be flunking his examinations so often. What about Sankar Sir? Did he abide by any discipline when he was young? Maybe the elders don't need any routine. But about one thing Banka was certain. After Sankar Sir broached the subject of the schedule he had felt a new surge of enthusiasm for his studies. Does one get more inspiration to work to become a good human being if one has faith in a system?

"Why are you meddling in others' affairs? What responsibility do you have to advise others' children? His parents are responsible for his welfare." Grandmother, who had come out of the prayer room after counting her beads, flung these words at Chacha. Banka knew that although she was chastising Chacha overtly, her jibe was in fact aimed at Mother. Grandmother had this habit of pampering Chacha. She spoiled for a fight if anyone even raised a little finger at him.

"Okay. We will never point out any of your mistakes," Chacha sulked.

"Give me money, I will fetch the paan and then prepare the timetable." Banka remembered Sankar Sir's dictum "the decision to be a good human being is under your control" even as he said this. To obey whatever your elders say, to do your work skilfully: are these the qualities of a good human being? But in this case when he obeys the elders he is unable to do his duties properly as a student. Banka was confused. He realised that it was not so easy to either become a good human being or do one's work skilfully. In every moment, in different contexts, the definition of a good human being and skilful work seemed to change. In this context, to go out and fetch paan might prevent a painful emotional storm that was brewing at home. After that he would tackle the task of routine-making at leisure.

When he came back from the shop Banka realised that he was not able to avert the storm as he had hoped. After finishing her cooking, Mother had gone to bed, claiming that she had a fast to observe. Whenever her words were not respected she resorted to this tactic of fasting. Father would try to assuage her feelings after returning from office. The emotions at home would hover at a flash point for a couple of days before gradually limping back to normal.

"Banka, come have your supper," Nani called out. Sometimes when Mother goes to bed early, Nani tended to his and Chhotu's needs.

Banka looked at the wall clock. It was 9 pm. There were only a few pencil-drawn lines on a piece of blank paper. Banka had not been able to make a decision regarding what subject he would study and when, what matters would be mentioned in the timetable and what withheld. The universal affection he had felt for the world around him a while ago was slowly receding from his consciousness. After finishing his meal Banka came back to his study-corner. He instructed his mind not to brood over things too deeply. He would just draw the lines and mention the subjects to be studied at random. Just to please Sankar Sir. But care should be taken that it does not look as outlandish as Hari's.

"The important thing is not the routine. The main thing is to study mindfully," Banka told himself. His hands and legs had started aching because of the amount of bowling he had done at the playground. After he washed down the meal with a glass of water, sleep suddenly engulfed him. But how could he go to bed before completing the timetable? If he went to bed at that time he was going to be rebuked by Father or Chacha. Moreover, if he did not complete the schedule during the night, how could he begin studying according to it? What would he show to Sankar Sir at school on Monday? Then he decided to work out a timetable only for Sunday. On Sunday night he would give more thought and prepare an elaborate routine for the whole week. The weight of sleep had become so heavy that he could not think of any other way. Between two parallel lines he perfunctorily wrote the following: Sunday (The Day for Self-evaluation): leave bed at 4 am. From 4 am to 5 am morning ablutions, meditation and reading of Hanuman Chalisa. Light breakfast by 5:30 am. From 5:30 am to 8.00 am solving one set of Mathematics questions from the test paper. From 8.00 am to 8.30 am proper breakfast and preparation for the next test. From 8:30 am to 10.00 am English test. From 10:30 am to 12:30 pm Social Sciences. From 12:30 pm to 1:30 pm lunch and nap. From 1:30 pm to 3:30 pm Science test. From 3:30 pm to 5.00 pm literature test. From 5.00 pm to 6.00 pm evening prayer and a short walk. From 6.00 pm to 8.00 pm Sanskrit test. From 8.30 pm to 9.00 pm assessing the result of the self-test and writing a detailed report on the day's performance in diary. The next half-hour has to be spent thinking about the work-schedule of the next week. At ten o'clock supper and then bed.

After writing this much Banka went near Mother's bed and said, "Mother please wake me up at 4 o'clock in the morning. I am going to sleep early today." If he did not tell Mother this who would protect him in a crisis? When Father or Chacha would ask why Banka had gone to bed so early when the exam was at hand who would give the proper explanation? He was filled with gratitude for Mother. On many such occasions Mother came to his rescue. Banka pretends that he wants to get up early in the morning. Mother takes him at his word. She actually wakes him up at 4 o'clock in the morning, even serves him a cup of hot tea to ward off sleep. Oh! How innocent mothers are! How easily they believe others! Banka drinks the cup of tea and goes back to bed and gets up two hours later just before Father wakes up.

Banka went to bed early but could not summon sleep. First because of the exertions on the cricket field, his shoulders and fingers were aching badly. Since he had overeaten, his stomach was heavy. His head had started reeling. A mild pain travelled from his neck to the end of his back. But the most important problem was the guilt of not having made a proper timetable, even for Sunday, as he had planned. If he could not fix even one day, how could he create order in the chaos of the coming days by means of the timetable? How could he do well in the exam? Build a career? Become a teacher? Marry Preeti?

Despite himself, Banka was overtaken by sleep. But it was not a peaceful sleep. Nightmares kept intruding on his sleep. Then a light sleep gripped him for a couple of minutes. During one of those periods of light sleep Banka dreamt he was visiting the zoo at Nandan Kanan. He and his companions were watching the animals in various enclosures. At one point, while travelling from one enclosure to another Banka realised that he had been separated from his friends. He had no clear idea who they were in the first place. But when he found himself alone, he discovered that he was imprisoned in one of the enclosures. A huge cage surrounded him. He was standing behind iron rods that crisscrossed each other. Those iron rods looked like pencil lines drawn on a plain white paper. Like the lines he had drawn to make the timetable. Inside the cage he remembered that in a few minutes the matric exam would begin. But Banka was unable to understand why he had come to visit the zoo instead of heading straight to the examination hall. But now the most difficult task was how to get to the examination hall on time, freeing himself from the strong iron bars of the cage. In great grief and anxiety his body became completely immobile. His sleep broke as he was in the act of praying desperately to Bajrangbali.

After he woke up he felt Chhotu's breath, he was sleeping beside him. Nani was also in deep sleep a little distance away. On another cot nearby, Grandfather was snoring loudly. On a sleeping mat on the floor his grandmother was also asleep. In her usual style she was growling while having an asthmatic bout. Once everything had become quiet, night had filled the atmosphere with its own peculiar sounds. The crickets were singing in unison one moment and then in the next were falling silent. Stars were blinking across the window railings. Everything was as it should be. He was lying on his bed, but during these hours Mother Earth might have travelled thousands of kilometres carrying him, these trees, shrubs and creepers, all those crickets, Nani, Chhotu, Grandfather, Grandmother, the mountains, rivers and streams, his school, Sankar Sir, Hari and even his darling Preeti. Kailash Sir, the geography teacher, once informed them that the Earth travels around nine hundred forty-two million kilometres on its axis in the course of three hundred sixty five days. Between the time when he started preparing the timetable and the present moment the Earth might have covered several thousand kilometres. But there seemed to be no dissonance anywhere. So why was he so troubled? What catastrophe would befall if he could not prepare the perfect timetable? Could the great time schedule of this universe not accommodate his slight imperfections, his minor aberrations? Banka felt a sense of extreme assurance. Then he fell back into a deep sleep.

# MONITOR

*Translated from "Monitor"*

When Robin Sir dropped his name in the class like a bombshell, Banka's heart missed a few beats. He was reminded of a poem by Wordsworth. A short poem of seven to eight lines, called "The Rainbow", whose very first line always baffled him. "My heart leaps up when I behold a rainbow in the sky." Bhagabat Sir, who taught English poetry, had tried hard to explain, but had failed to drive home the point. How can the heart leap when one saw a rainbow? The heart is supposed to stay fixed, fenced in by the ribs. How can it leap? Can a human being survive if the heart actually leapt? As it was, he did not do well in literature. But after he joined the new school, the headmaster Kailash Sir came down to their house and started teaching him English and Sanskrit himself. He supposedly did that because he was a friend of Father's. Moreover, he believed that Banka could be among the top ten students of the state in the matriculation examination. For long, no one from the school had made it into that hallowed list. If Banka were crowned with that rare honour, the school would be glorified, the prestige of the teachers would be enhanced. With this idea of the school gaining a competitive advantage, Kailash Sir placed him under his personal tutelage.

Though Banka had failed to top after six months of direct guidance, he had somehow developed a liking for literature. He had been placed in section C provisionally because he had been admitted to the school in the middle of the academic session. But by the time teaching for class ten began, Banka had been shifted to section A, in which the most meritorious students of the class were placed. The teachers made their best efforts for the students of that section. There was special coaching for them even on Sundays and other holidays. The teachers took turns to identify their weaknesses and tried to address them. Whoever had any doubt had a chance to clarify them in these extra hours of teaching. The headmaster, Kailash Sir, himself oversaw these efforts, started a year in advance, to ensure that all the students of that section cleared the matriculation examination with a first class.

Banka considered himself fortunate for being brought to that section. For there was a sense of veneration in the entire school for section A of class ten and class eleven. But when Robin Sir was made the class teacher of their section, all the students, including Banka, were both surprised and frustrated. Not that Robin Sir had any deficiency as a teacher. He was one of the few teachers with an M.A. degree after Upadhyay Sir left the school on being selected as a judge in a local court. But he had this slightly negative reputation as a loud-mouth. As it was, he had this unconventional name which sounded like that of Bandit Robin, the famous hero of a popular detective novel series by Jogindra Das. On top of that he was not very particular about taking classes. He rode his motorcycle to the school in a pair of jeans and a t-shirt, and with a pair of dark glasses over his eyes. He was often seen smoking cigarettes near the staff common room. This type of conduct for a teacher was not palatable for many in the small backward town where Banka lived. The tales of his political clout and moneyed background gave him some immunity no doubt, but the mismatch between his flippant personality and the gravitas expected of a class teacher of section A of class ten was hard to ignore.

"Yesterday the ministry was formed. Our Krushna babu got the portfolio of Labour," Robin Sir announced dramatically after taking the attendance. Banka could easily see that this announcement was made to augment Robin Sir's own sense of importance. As if he was letting the students realise how close he was to Krushna babu MLA, how privy he was to some of the most important happenings of the state, like the formation of the ministry, despite being a nondescript teacher of a mere municipal school. But nobody could grudge his forays into current politics because it came under the ambit of the subjects he taught: civics and general knowledge. In Banka's friend circle an impression had been created that good students should become IAS officers when they grew up. And to clear the IAS examination your general knowledge had to be excellent. Therefore the jeans-clad, goggles-wearing, stylish hair-sporting, chain-smoking Robin Sir was profoundly relevant.

"And Biju Patnaik?" Banka asked inadvertently. He had great respect for the adventurous lifestyle of Biju Patnaik.

"What about Biju Patnaik? He would be the honorable leader of the opposition." Robin Sir answered with slightly less enthusiasm.

The fact that this bloody lecher Krushna, who had eloped with a minor girl of this very school ten years ago, would become a minister, and a charismatic personality like Biju Patnaik would sit in the opposition was anathema to Banka. "Sir, you were there when the ministry was formed. Why didn't you try to get something for Biju Patnaik?" Banka asked.

"Arrey, people's opinion is the most valuable thing in a democracy. People wanted Biju babu to remain in the opposition, not become a minister. What could we do? For example, if all the students opine that Bankanidhi Harichandan should become the monitor of this class, should we not accept that opinion with our heads bowed?" Robin Sir was trying to change the subject.

That was when Banka's heart took a sudden leap. His body froze. In a strange gush of emotion his body was shaken to its hair follicles. His tongue felt dry inside his parched mouth. In a flash he understood the meaning of the poem "The Rainbow" by Wordsworth, which he had been unable to understand for a month. Thoroughly flabbergasted, he continued to stand although he should have taken his seat after asking the question.

"Then what is your democratic opinion? Those who want Bankanidhi to be the monitor of this class please raise your hands," Robin Sir ordered.

From the corner of his eyes Banka saw the backbenchers raising their hands with alacrity. They probably surmised it was Robin Sir's desire to choose Banka as the monitor, and going against the wishes of the class teacher was not a wise decision. Attendance, fines, progress reports, etc., were all in his hands. If the teacher was favorable then there would be no fear of getting fined if you were caught cutting school to watch the occasional matinee show. Imitating the backbenchers, the boys sitting on the middle benches also raised their hands. These boys did not have the ability to think independently. They preferred to drift with the current. But the brightest boys and most beautiful girls of the class in the front seats were still undecided. Their number was miniscule compared to the total strength of the class. But their voice carried more weight. Among the students and teachers, both. Prithiviraj, who topped the class, was also among the brightest front benchers. Prithiviraj was as handsome as he was good at studies. Moreover, since he was an old student of the school he had a devoted fan club. The entire group excelled both in studies and mischief. During lunch-break they smoked behind the Mahadev temple, placed anonymous love letters in the books of female students, went to matinee shows during school hours and so on. It was probably for this reason Robin Sir broke with the tradition of selecting the topper as class monitor and chose the timid and quiet Banka, though he had joined the school only six months ago.

"Now how many are in support of Bankanidhi..." As soon as Robin Sir said this, Banka saw Prithiviraj's hand go up. He was smart. He had calculated by that time that only a few students had not raised their hands. He must have reckoned that it was to his advantage to remain in the good books of the class teacher. But once they saw Prithiviraj raising his hand all his hangers-on raised their hands. All the girls too.

The civics teacher Robin Sir didn't have to do any arithmetic. "Okay, then by the unanimous decision of this class Bankanidhi is declared as the class monitor."

The announcement was received with clapping, some genuine and some not so genuine. After the clapping died down Robin Sir again announced, "Congratulations, Bankanidhi. Now it is your job to shoulder the responsibility efficiently. This is how the foundation of leadership is laid. It is up to you to prove whether you are worthy of the role."

After Robin Sir left the class, it was Prithiviraj who came up to him first to congratulate him. Six months ago, when he first came to the school, it was Prithiviraj who had come up to him first to greet him. It was also he who made his life miserable with his banter. He was chosen as monitor because he topped the class. Not to speak of maintaining discipline, he was instrumental in breaking all discipline not only in his own section A but also in Banka's section where he was placed temporarily. He encouraged smoking and watching matinee shows when students got together during recess. Since Banka never fell into his trap he showered him with derogatory adjectives like "halu" (moron), "mafa" (rustic), "super fine chuda" (idiot of the first order), etc. Banka could understand that this was a well-thought-out plan. On the inside, Prithiviraj was afraid of the possibility of the timid, reticent, disciplined and studious Banka becoming the topper of the class. Like planning a move in a game of chess, Prithiviraj was trying to demoralise him psychologically. Although he did not share this with anyone, Banka understood his designs well. He could also detect the fear lurking beneath Prithiviraj's aggressiveness. Contrarily, the competitive attitude to top the class, be among the top ten students in the matriculation, could never inspire Banka. His own fears, doubts, and sloth so enveloped him that the pranks of Prithiviraj and his ilk appeared rather childish to him.

"What are you ruminating over so much?" Prithiviraj assured. "Why are you apprehensive? We are there. We will see to it that things get done well. You'll see Harichandan, class Ten A will be the best in all the competitions this year."

In fact, the school tradition had it that various competitions, like decoration of the classroom, painting and handicraft exhibition, debate, essay and short story writing, singing and music, etc., were held during

Republic Day and Independence Day celebrations. On these occasions the monitor of the class that received the most prizes, was felicitated by the school. Thus the monitor had a useful role in inspiring his class to win more and more prizes.

Prithiviraj was hinting at those prizes. The monitor had to decide which student would represent the class in what competition. Prithiviraj wanted to represent the class in maximum number of competitions so he was trying to curry Banka's favour. Banka could well understand the meaning of Prithiviraj's flattery. But he did not say anything. He was thinking about something else. About Robin Sir and the so-called majority opinion in a democracy. Was this the face of public opinion and democracy? Robin Sir did not want to make Prithiviraj or anyone from his coterie the monitor of this class, so without alerting anybody about his intentions he conducted the election for the monitor. He imposed an unassertive boy like him on the class. Be it for weaknesses or for fear of the teacher, everyone accepted the decision even though Banka had not demonstrated any leadership ability. The joyous feeling that had flitted through his mind after being elected as monitor started receding. He thought whatever happened in his class must happen everywhere else. Otherwise, how did the lecher Krushna become a minister while Biju Patnaik sat in the opposition?

This thought continued to trouble Banka even at home. At first he had thought he would startle Nani with the news of his selection as the monitor when she came back from college. Sharing the news would be revenge for Nani's usual habit of running down his abilities. Then he would distribute chocolates among his friends in the cricket team. But when he recollected the entire process through which he was made the monitor he did not feel like sharing the information even with Chhotu. After a long deliberation he just managed to whisper to his mother, "Bou, I have been made the monitor of the class."

Mother, who got excited even by Banka's negligible achievements, responded absentmindedly, "Have you? Good, good." Probably because she was busy cooking.

But when Father came back from office she communicated the news with considerable enthusiasm, "You know, our Banka has become the monitor of his class."

Father said, "How do I know? Am I omniscient? Matric exam is in the offing. One should focus on studies. What would one get by becoming the monitor? He does not have any goal for himself. In the previous school he used to top the class. Here he could not even be among the top five. That too, after such close attention by Kailash Sir."

Father had this habit of diluting the importance of everything. He was never content with what he had. It was in his nature to remain discontented, thinking about what he did not have. He asked, "Hey Banka, you have become the monitor of your class?" Whatever he had said to Bou had already killed his spirit. So Banka just nodded unenthusiastically.

Father then asked, "Tell me, what is the meaning of the word monitor."

This was another of Father's problems. He would ask such uncomfortable questions in the presence of everybody in such a manner that you would be completely stumped. Lest Father was humiliated in front of his friends, Banka had memorised the names of the capital cities of almost a hundred countries from Namibia to Zambia. He had also noted down thousands of scientific innovations, the names of thousands of great authors of world literature, the dates of birth and death of great men, and would go over them every once in a while.

He had earned his reputation as a bright student by answering Father's questions promptly in the presence of his friends. His father might be getting some satisfaction from that, but Banka felt terribly bored. Therefore, he had resolved not to answer such questions, but out of habit he blurted out, "According to Oxford dictionary, a school pupil with disciplinary or other special duties."

Banka had already checked the dictionary, anticipating such a question. Father seemed happy. Although Banka didn't feel like making his father happy at that moment, he gave the correct answer out of habit.

Father said, "It is alright. Become the monitor. Nobody is stopping you. But you should never forget your aim, your swadharma."

He continued to reel out slogans from the Gita and nuggets of wisdom from the works of Vivekananda but nothing seemed to enter Banka's ears. To offer such dry, pointless advice was Father's nature, probably his swadharma. Then what was Banka's swadharma? How could he know what his swadharma was? Does a human being know what his swadharma is from the moment of his birth? Or does one have to accept what Father or Robin Sir or Kailash Sir gave out as his swadharma? Ideally one should weigh all his experiences and examine them against one's own nature before identifying one's swadharma. But life's tenure might be over while one was going through this process. By the time one identifies one's swadharma there would be hardly enough time left to organise one's life around it.

These thoughts continued to confuse Banka. About one thing he was, however, certain: the ideas and ideals in the Shastras and Puranas were meant to befuddle the mind. To live those ideals was hardly easy. He had never seen his grandma practise any of the ideals she might be coming across while reading her Puranas daily. The gap between Grandma's deeds and the words of the Puranas had turned Banka away from those Puranas. Nani and Chhotu kept listening to the stories from the Puranas from Grandma, but Banka had completely lost interest in them.

Then are these ideals false? Or maybe great men had the ability to live the ideals, for that reason they became great men. Like Vivekananda. But Banka had no interest in emulating Vivekananda. Vivekananda was a celibate all his life. From the day Banka had seen Sangita, the thought of celibacy had vanished from his mind. She was the daughter of Mishra Uncle, a friend of Father's. She studied in class seven. She lived just behind Banka's house. Probably for lack of any friends, Sangita always hovered around Nani. They always gossiped in hushed tones about god knows what. She lowered her eyes whenever she came across Banka. And the day Mother told Mishra Aunty jokingly that she would get this girl as her daughter-in-law, Banka decided that he would never follow the ideals of Swami Vivekananda. After reading Vivekananda's Chicago speech he had thought that the path chosen by the Swami should be his swadharma. But over the last six months, and especially after meeting Sangita, he had been looking for a different swadharma. Maybe the path of Vivekananda was too out of reach, but he could at least set a new benchmark as the monitor of the class. Transcending the limits of an ordinary monitor he could create a special identity for himself. Not only his classmates, or Kailash Sir or Robin Sir, even his father would be dazzled by his actions. And Sangita...

The next day, Banka called the roll from the attendance register after recess. This was one of the monitor's duties. The class teacher takes the attendance in the first period. After recess the monitor has to report whether all the students are present or not. Truants, if any, were fined. That day everyone was present. After taking attendance Banka announced, "Brothers and Sisters". The commotion of taking attendance stopped. The students had not reckoned that a monitor would start delivering a speech like a politician. They looked at Banka with curiosity, but Banka was in a complete funk by then. He was normally a shy boy, even while taking attendance his hands had trembled out of nervousness. Because of the decision he had taken the previous night to give a speech on his first day as monitor, he blurted out the address "Brothers and Sisters." But his mouth felt dry with fear, and he forgot the speech he had planned throughout the night. Then he remembered Vivekananda's Chicago address "Brothers and Sisters of America", and he was filled with courage. Emboldened, he spewed out, "We celebrate Ganesh Puja and Saraswati Puja every year. We clean up our surroundings on the School Foundation Day, Independence Day and Republic Day. Students win prizes in various competitions. The prestige of our class is enhanced because of this. We accomplish all these in accordance with the traditions of the past. I am not saying that we should not engage in these. Identity and sense of glory are essential for us. But not merely in the directions set by society. We have to build our identity by going beyond what is handed down to us. That would be the real test of our character. Whether our glory will be enhanced by that, I don't know. But only by facing a new challenge can we discover ourselves. My suggestion is that during recess we should put up a fence around our playground. That would be the real demonstration of what we can achieve if we put our shoulders to the wheel."

There was enthusiastic clapping after Banka's speech. But he noticed that Prithiviraj and his followers appeared crestfallen. Prithiviraj went so far as to whisper to a boy near him words of insinuation meant for Banka's ears, "Bloody Robin master has gifted this to him and this slip of a boy thinks he has become a governor. Seems he will become an MLA after Krushna Pradhan."

Prithiviraj's words encouraged his acolytes to make fun of Banka. But he went to his seat unmindful of all this. He had felt the necessity of such a fence for a long time. When they played cricket, the ball often travelled to spots on the field that were covered with wild shrubs. On one side of the playground there were the school's buildings, on another the main street of the town, the third side housed an electric substation and its long boundary wall. Only one side of the playground was unprotected, taking advantage of which the people of the local basti used the space for their morning ablutions. One had to be very careful searching for the ball in the shrub, thorny bushes of berries and fresh excreta. Banka felt so revolted that he stopped playing cricket at school. Although cricket was the sport dearest to his heart. He was so fond of cricket that he thought more about the game than he did about Sangita. This idea of building a fence crept into his mind because of his love for cricket. He reckoned that if a strong fence was erected around the ground the local people would not be able to use it as a latrine. Moreover, the ball could not travel across the fence towards the wild shrubbery. Of course, there were plans to fence the school playground. The municipality too had earmarked funds for a permanent wall. But since the people of the local community were using the ground as a pathway they were opposing any permanent structure. If a wall was erected they would have to take a detour of an extra mile to reach the highway. The local councilor, dependent upon the votes of those people, had stalled the proposal to erect a wall a couple of times by putting pressure on the headmaster and the governing body of the school.

Banka and his friends in the class were unaware of this history. So, from the next day they started putting together a fence with great enthusiasm. Even Haria, who used that space for smoking bidis and defecating after school hours, led the drive for collecting donations. With the tacit support of Robin Sir, poles, nails, bamboos, wires and crowbars were bought. Students volunteered their labour enthusiastically. In a couple of days they had covered half of the huge ground. Despite his assurances Prithiviraj and his group were absolutely uncooperative. But Banka was unfazed. An unknown confidence and courage had taken hold of his mind. The kind of fear and hesitance he had felt when he first came to the new school was replaced with bubbling enthusiasm. His zest for work had spread like a contagion and the others devoted themselves to the work wholeheartedly. It appeared as if the entire task would be accomplished in four to five days. Now they would have a safe playground. Not just the students of Banka's class but future students too would benefit from this deed. While playing in the field, they would remember Banka and his friends with such love and devotion!

This thought had so engrossed him that he hardly felt hunger and thirst. Whenever he sat down to study after evening prayers he could not see the printed letters. When he opened a book the picture of the playground flashed across his mind. In his imagination he likened the future of the school playground with the green velvety grounds of Barabati Stadium where he had watched the three-day cricket match between East Zone and the West Indies. Why couldn't the school ground become like the Barabati lawns? Suddenly, Father's shout cut into his reverie.

"Hey, Banka, come here."

Banka hurried from his study table to the drawing room.

Banka had not realised that Father was back from work and was having tea.

"What are you doing? Didn't you hear my call?" Father said.

Banka was apprehensive. This kind of call in the middle of study hour portended bad weather, in the form of a severe beating. But he could not remember any mischief he had done which called for a beating. But if Nani or Chhotu had filled his ears with something, then it would be a different matter. In that case the volume of beating would be small. Banka desperately wished for Mother's presence. During Grandma's absence, Mother was the only saviour against the fury of Father's punishment.

"Studying," Banka was laconic.

"What were you studying? The teachers reported to me that you are more inclined towards extra-curricular activities these days? Have you forgotten your goal? The headmaster is of the opinion that if you stick to your goal you can come within the top ten students in matriculation examination. Look, the four ensuing years is the time for hard work. In these years it will be decided whether you are a horse of a long race or, like scores of others, an ordinary ass. Go, concentrate on your studies. Don't let me receive any more complaints from the teachers."

Heaving a sigh of relief Banka thanked Bajrangbali. He also promised two bananas as offerings the next day at the nearby Hanuman temple.

Of course, he had completely forgotten about the offering the next morning. Only one thought occupied his mind. How to concentrate on studies as soon as the fencing work was finished. There should not be any scope for complaint from the teachers. But in the first period itself all his calculations vanished into thin air. Bhagabat Sir, the English teacher, appeared in the class in lieu of Robin Sir, the class teacher. First he read out a notice from the headmaster which said that henceforth Bhagabat Sir would be the class teacher in place of Robin Sir. After taking attendance Bhagabat Sir asked, "Who stood first in class in the last annual examination?"

With great pride Prithiviraj stood up from his seat.

"Are you the monitor of this class?" Bhagabat Sir probed further.

Slightly offended, Prithiviraj looked at Banka from the corner of his eyes and mumbled "No, Sir."

"Why? According to the tradition of the school, the student who comes first in the previous examination should become the monitor of the class. From today you are the monitor of this class. Does anyone have anything to say on this?" Bhagabat Sir asked.

Prithiviraj's lackeys cried enthusiastically, "No Sir."

They then followed this up with clapping, hailing the decision. Banka was perplexed with this sudden turn of events. Prithiviraj was smiling at him as if he had conquered a fort in a battle. Banka was so humiliated that he hoped he would be swallowed by the earth, leaving no trace like Sita of Ramayana. He glanced furtively at the students who had helped him a lot in erecting the fence. But who would contradict such a strict teacher like Bhagabat Sir? Moreover, Bhagabat Sir was the assistant headmaster of the school.

Perfect silence reigned in the classroom. None of what Bhagabat Sir taught that day entered Banka's ears. He was preparing to get himself under control after the class. The banter of the front bench girls was no big deal. The hardest part was having to face Prithiviraj. The moment the class was over and before anybody could understand what was going on Banka got up from his seat, walked to Prithiviraj and embraced him.

"Brother, you saved me. You should have become the monitor. I don't know why Robin Sir trapped me into this. Since becoming the monitor I have been beaten up every evening at home. Father has repeatedly requested the headmaster to relieve me of this. Now you take the responsibility. We will all support you."

Prithiviraj knew Banka's father was a well-placed government official. He had good relations with all the teachers. Banka wanted Prithiviraj to know that the reversal of Robin Sir's decision was not a defeat for him, but was stage-managed by Banka's father in collaboration with the teachers. This was a desperate effort from Banka to gain some psychological compensation for the deep humiliation he had suffered.

With the traditional magnanimity of the victor, Prithiviraj embraced him and answered, "Arrey, I will be monitor in name only. You will remain the real monitor. Your father and teachers will never come to know about it. But you must stop the fencing work on the ground. I have heard that the Krushna Pradhan's lackey, who has become the councillor of this ward, does not want a fence around the school playground. He has probably put pressure on the headmaster for this."

Placing an arm on his shoulder Prithiviraj led him out of the class.

He said, "There is another request. On the days I bunk classes to go watch a matinee show you should take the attendance. If somebody tries to tell on me, just tell the class teacher that I have suddenly taken ill."

Banka remembered his grandma narrating a tale from the Puranas. While the gods and demons churned the sea, there surfaced both nectar and poison. All were vying with each other to drink the nectar while the poison was threatening to destroy the entire Creation. Fortunately, Lord Shiva was around. When he was summoned, he gulped down all the poison, and Creation was saved. Shiva drank the poison alright but it did not go past his throat, so his throat became blue. He earned the sobriquet of Nilakantha—the one with a blue throat. But Banka felt that Shiva was not coming forward anymore to save Banka's small world. Here every drop of nectar was laced with a droplet of poison.

# INITIATION

*Translated from "Khadichhuan"*

Banka felt upbeat after the notice was read out in class that day. It reminded him of last year's promise. Last year too, such a notice by the headmaster to submit articles for the school magazine had been read out in Mathematics class. After sending back the peon who had brought the notice, the Mathematics teacher had gone back to the blackboard to explain the geometry theorem. Banka also had not given much importance to that notice, there being nothing to differentiate it from countless other such notices issued by the headmaster. But when the school magazine was published, he was startled to find an article under his name towards the end of the volume. Someone else must have written the article in his name. That too, in English. It was a collection of some of the famous sayings by great men across human history. His own name appeared as the compiler of those sayings.

It must be the hard work of Kailash Sir who had edited the magazine. Kailash Sir happened to be a friend of Father. He might not have liked the idea that the magazine would publish articles by other students but would not feature the name of Banka. That was why he might have cobbled together various sayings and attributed them to him. But apparently nobody else had known about it. Mother was happy about it. Though Nani was outwardly dismissive, she read his article surreptitiously. Boys like Chandrabhanu and Janmejoy, who borrowed huge English novels during the library hour just to impress the girls, burnt with envy.

The article was not ordinary. It was placed in the English section of the magazine, where only articles by the teachers were published. The first article in that section was under his name. The day after the magazine was circulated among the students, Nibedita, the most beautiful girl of the class, smiled at him while reading his article during the lunch-break. Banka felt his chest expand in joy. Of course he was reminded once in a while of Nani's words of suspicion, "You rascal, you must have stolen someone else's writing. When did you write it? Why, I have not seen you writing this one!" Although he was irritated with Nani, he felt weak inside. Nani, after all, was telling the truth. Even though others did not know, he himself knew that the article was not written by him. Had Nani shared her suspicion with Nibedita? Was Nibedita's smile meant to mock him? Was she looking at him from the corner of her eyes because she had found out about his cheating?

The pleasure of seeing his own name in print ended in a day. The article felt like a huge burden on his shoulders. He was silently angry with Kailash Sir. What was the need for all this? Was it so necessary for his name to appear in the school magazine just because he was a good student? Even if his name appeared, why did it have to be published in the English section? People were suspicious precisely because of its placement in the English section. As it was, nobody ever read the articles of the teachers published in it. They were solemn essays on "How to become a good student", "What is the aim of human life", "Duties of a good student" and so on. At the very end there would be a bunch of advice by the headmaster. Who would bother with reading them? However, that section carried the maximum prestige. He was as happy at his name appearing in that section as he was disturbed at not having written that article himself. He vowed to himself that next year he would write an article for the school magazine. When it was published, he would nonchalantly throw a copy in Nani's face. He would prove to Chandrabhanu, Janmejoy and others that he was not just a class topper in studies but could also write, participate in sports, and debate competitions. If Nibedita stole a glance at him, he would go straight to her and ask whether she liked his article. He would also declare that he already had hundreds of such articles in his diary, and, if she was interested he would love to share them with her.

Like all vows he forgot about this one too, as time went by. The headmaster's notice was circulated again. This time in the period allotted to Nanda Sir. Stopping midway in his teaching of literature, he read the notice in original English. After sending back the notice with the peon he took a long time interpreting it in Odia. It was curtains for the literature lesson.

Nanda Sir then went on to explain how the school magazine was a reflection of the creative potential of the students; how creativity was fundamental to being human; how it helped transcend one's own ego in order to have a taste of the bliss of liberation. It did not matter whether the students understood what the teacher was saying, they were happy because teaching stopped abruptly. But Nanda Sir's last few words reminded Banka of the vow he had made a year ago. These words told him that while success in examination and success in life as defined by society were necessary, they were not the be all and end all.

To make man and his society more beautiful and divine one needed to go beyond social success, Nanda Sir said. Creativity was the real vehicle to embark upon for such a journey. Then Nanda Sir presented several examples from the life history of writers from the literature textbook. They may not have been outwardly successful, but were able to show mankind the horizon of new possibilities through their creativity.

Banka felt as if Nanda Sir's words were directed at him. He scored very good marks in all the subjects but never did well in literature. So he had never been his favourite.

When Nanda Sir had asked him about his aim in

life, he had declared that he wanted to study engineering at IIT and then go to America. Everyone had laughed at his words. Nanda Sir, however, had gravely replied that becoming a good human being required more effort than becoming a successful one. Was he retorting to his declared ambition of going to America? Whatever it might be, he would write an article for this year's magazine. He would prove that a good human being also needed to be successful occasionally. The student that topped the class could also be creative. Apart from all this, Nibedita at least would have the proof of his ability for creative expression. Pramila—he suddenly remembered Pramila, his flame in the school at Cuttack which he had left to come to a school in Choudwar—would also come to know that his article had been published in the school magazine.

Banka hurried home as soon as school ended. His four pm playtime had been suspended due to the approaching matriculation examination. After the evening meal he took a stroll along the river bank. Then, as per the timetable, he sat down to prepare for the examination at exactly six o'clock, after a quick evening prayer. Chacha had laid down a minute-to-minute routine for him. Although he himself had failed thrice in his own B.A. examination, he was quite vigilant about Banka's studies. From 6.00 in the evening to 7:15 he studied Mathematics, from 7:15 to 8.00 pm English, from 8.00 to 8:30 Science, from 8:30 to 9.00 Social Science and from 9.00 to 9:30 he had to devote himself to optional subjects. During the holidays he had to revise the Sanskrit and Odia lessons. Chacha was on him like a leech. Leaving all his other work, he was tracking Banka's movements with great enthusiasm. Banka felt suffocated but had no other option, for Mother and Nani were on Chacha's side in the matter of his preparations for examination. He felt a new lease of life after the notice was read out that day.

Reaching home, he quickly gulped down a little rice and got up. He was usually terribly hungry at that time, but that day Banka had no time to think about his hunger. After the hasty meal he went straight to the study room and sat down, spreading a mat on the floor. For some reason he picked up the timetable Chacha had prepared, squeezed it into a paper ball and threw it out of the window. He felt a surge of courage. He had an answer ready for any possible enquiry by Chacha about his studies. He could give a straight answer that Nanda Sir had asked him to write an article within three to four days for the school annual magazine. So, all regular studies would have to be suspended for the time being. He had full faith that if Chacha tried to play any trick or put up any obstacle he could take the matter to Father through Kailash Sir.

After throwing away the timetable and picking up a pen and a bunch of papers he sat down with great conviction to write an article; but what would he write? First he leafed through last year's school magazine. Then he picked up Father's favourite journal *Jhankara.* There were several short stories, essays and poems in its pages.

What should he write? A short story? An essay? A poem or something else? Should he write the kind of articles the teachers wrote for the English section, in Odia? Full of advice about the responsibilities of a good student? Bloody hell, who would read such articles? Those were tolerated just because the teachers wrote them. If he wrote that kind of article in Odia he would end up being ridiculed. Girls like Nibedita would scoff at them. Should he write something like the essays that were set in question papers for the examinations, like an essay on "flood" or "cow"? No, not at all. Everybody wrote answers to such questions, but they were not fit subjects for journals. As Nanda Sir had said, the writings needed to be creative. Like those that found a place in literature textbooks, something new, the kind of writing that broke with whatever had been written so far. It would use the same words, the same language but would appear new to readers. Like the kind of stuff Faka, the tailor's son, sometimes wrote. The rogue wrote the couplets, imitating the nine-lettered metre of the holy Bhagabata and recited these in their presence:

> The good and bad sides of a living being
> Can be known at the time of their shagging

The writer of the Bhagabata had meant that the qualities of a human being could be known at the time of their death; but the naughty Faka parodied even such high philosophy in his own inimitable vulgar style. His parody tickled his audience to no end. Not only that, he had made erotic parodies of several tales of holy texts like the Ramayana and the Mahabharata. Faka was not a very good student, but what a creative talent he was!

Should he, too, write such a blasphemous poem? Was anything new, novel, creative? Another thing: creative or not, the teachers would not publish such articles. Otherwise Faka could also have submitted them for the school journal. There was more danger if by chance such an article somehow got published and came to the notice of his family members. Not only Chacha or Mother, even Father would thrash him mercilessly for writing such stuff. Once his friend Rabi was passing by their house, carrying two books by Mastram, the famous writer of dirty books. Unfortunately, Father's eyes fell on them. He snatched the books away from Rabi and slapped Banka so hard that he fell down like a tree uprooted by a storm. Father did not stop there. Rabi was asked to come to their house with his father next morning. Then began Banka's thrashing in their presence, for half an hour. Banka's entreaties that he had not read the books fell on deaf ears. His mistake was that he had befriended someone like Rabi and that Rabi had turned up at their house on a Sunday. Banka could not figure out how to explain Rabi's motives. The thrashing on that occasion was so severe that even Chacha took his side and dragged him away from that place. Chacha then showered him with advice throughout the evening on how to become a good human being and not befriend bad boys, and so on. That advice was like rubbing salt into the wounds caused by the thrashing.

Should he write a short story, then, if he could not write an erotically charged parody? Everyone would love to read a story. He, too, loved a good story, about the old she-demon or about the kings and queens, the damsel with long hair, the cunning flower-woman, the tale of four bosom friends or the myna who talked like humans or about flying saucers.

But those stories had already been written. What more could he write about them? Those who were writing in *Jhankara* were also not writing about kings or queens anymore, so why should he? Should he write a story about the prime minister or chief minister? But what did he know about them? Last year the chief minister had come for the school's annual prize-giving ceremony, and after giving his inaugural address he quickly left, citing some other important appointment. Banka had seen him only from a distance for ten or fifteen minutes, sweating heavily on that scorching day. Could one write a story or a poem or an essay on the basis of such a flimsy experience?

As it was, what did he know about anybody or anything? As a child he had seen the sarpanch, the village head at close quarters. During summer vacation they had gone to their ancestral village with Chacha. The panchayat election had just ended. After the declaration of results they were taking the winning candidate in a procession. The plump man with a few garlands of currency notes and flowers around his neck was leading the crowd of supporters. A few supporters were chanting

"Hail the victor" while a few others were playing pipes and drums. When they passed in front of their house, a few children of their locality started shouting "Hail the victorious Biren Palei". Banka didn't know what got into him at that time, and he too ran alongside those children shouting the same slogan even as his grandmother was trying to restrain him. As he came very close to the plump man, the latter stretched out his hand and touched his head as a gesture of blessing. Then he joined his palms to greet the women standing in their respective verandas. When Grandma narrated the incident to Chacha, the thrashing started. Not only was the thrashing severe, the incident occasioned their early return home, shortening their vacation. When the matter was reported at home there was fresh abuse and punishment. That was not so bad, but Banka dearly missed the annual Ramlila yatra, feasting upon mangoes in the orchard, roaming around the huge yard, and playing on the swing during the Raja festival which they enjoyed every summer.

At home they were back to the usual routine of school days: getting up at first light, finishing morning ablutions, prayer, and studies. There was some respite during the afternoon when you were allowed to play in the field at the end of the street. But again, you had to come back home before evening. The ordeal with the home tutor would begin directly after finishing prayer. The tutor would give them so much homework that Banka often failed to complete it before dinner. By the time dinner was over, his lids would be heavy with sleep.

Only on Mondays they were allowed to listen to the radio drama at 9 pm. With such a rigorous regime what would Banka know that he could shape into an article? The only instruction Banka ever got was "study", "study more", "study more and more". It was not enough to stand first in your section or in the whole class. Scoring eighty or ninety per cent was not enough. He was supposed to do well in the final examination to be placed among the top ten students of the entire province. This was the only tune everyone sang, be it Father, Mother, Chacha, Nani, the teachers, the headmaster, everyone.

Whatever little he knew about the world was from the story books he was allowed to read on Sundays. From those books Banka knew that there was a larger world beyond school, home, the field at the end of the street, the long vacation in the village, his adult guardians, brothers and sisters and teachers. Sometimes he felt envious of Tom Sawyer, Huck Finn, the Little Prince, Alibaba, Abolkara, etc. The raft in the Mississippi river, Aladdin's magic lamp, the magician's flying carpet, were all these stories true? His childhood was about to run its course. When would he experience these things? If he did not experience them, what would he write about? It looked like he would have to write something on his own steam. Not following the articles in the school magazine, or *Jhankara*, or other books or because of Kailash Sir's indulgence.

He desperately longed to experience the larger world beyond the veranda of his home, the street full of speeding vehicles, the field at the end of the street and Nibedita's smile. He would frame that experience within a measured, disciplined language and serve it to the world. Thrilled by that articulation himself he would be able to provide the Sunday joy to those who like him were on the quest for that divinity in words.

Pummm...pummmm...pummm...pum. He heard Mother blowing the conch for evening prayer, three long sounds followed by a half. Banka had not noticed evening fall. He slapped his cheek on feeling a burning sensation. His fingers were smeared with the blood of two mosquitoes he had crushed. They were bloated with his blood and he had not felt them bite him. Now he had to go for prayer. Suddenly, in the semi-darkness of dusk he saw that something was written on the plain paper he had placed before him for his composition. But he had not written anything yet. The pen he had uncapped was still lying unused. Then what were the characters on the plain paper? He immediately got up and switched on the tube light. No, there was nothing. In the bright light he saw that the plain paper and the uncapped pen were as he had left them. The characters he had seen on the paper were a trick of the eyes in the semi-darkness.

The smell of burning camphor and sandalwood incense sticks came wafting across from the prayer room, Banka hurried towards it. Mother was still ringing the bell. Nani's prayer would commence as soon as the bell stopped. There would be trouble if he was not present before the bell stopped ringing. Mother's aarti was going on in front of the figures of the gods and goddesses. The small flame in the lamp looked like a yellow drop of water. The sound of the cackling birds floated in intermittently from the huge banyan tree near the field at the end of the street. The sound of the birds could be heard every day; aarti was offered; the bell was rung; the conch-shell was blown; Nani recited a prayer; Banka and Chhotu followed Nani's lead; the still light of the lamp brightened the prayer room; the place was filled with the scent of the camphor and incense sticks. To Banka it seemed as if he was experiencing all these things for the first time. He was looking at the world anew. The blank sheet of paper, the uncapped pen, the school, the perimeter of his house, the thrashings and abuses, the anger, frustration and envy, Nibedita's smile, Nanda Sir's advice, everything appeared meaningful to him. He also felt as if all thoughts had been drained from his mind. Only one thought—that he would not be able to write an article for the school magazine after all—flashed once in a while in the vacuum of his mind. But that thought somehow emboldened him instead of making him nervous. The instinct that had prompted him to crumple the timetable and toss it away, and made him resolve to prove himself to Nanda Sir, was becoming more articulate by the minute. An unknown joy overwhelmed his mind. That joy pushed his inability to write to the background. In an enchanted state Banka finished his prayer. After finishing his homework he had his dinner.

In the night he had a strange dream; he had become an adult just like Father, Chacha and his schoolteachers. He was wearing pants, shirt, socks, and shoes just like them.

But, strangely, it was the occasion of his Khadichhuan—a rite of initiation—which was normally solemnised at the Ugratara temple in their village, and had taken place a long time ago, during his early childhood. The ends of his ears were pierced first with a silver needle, next with a gold needle, and finally with a steel needle and a cotton thread was tied like a ring through the piercing. When his ears were pierced by the steel needle Grandma shoved a huge sweetmeat into his mouth so that he could not cry in pain. (Oh my God, what a nuisance it would have been for an adult to cry!) By the time he gulped down the sweetmeat the village abadhana—teacher—handed a huge piece of chalk to him. Holding his fingers and palm he made him draw three circles on the black slate in front of him. While making him trace the circles again and again he was calling out loudly the names of Brahma, Vishnu and Maheswara. Although Banka had already become an adult he was unable to understand why the three similar looking circles had three different names. The first name was for the creator, the middle one for the preserver and the last one for the destroyer. But how was it that all three were big zeroes?

At this moment of confusion he woke up. It was Sunday morning. After his morning ablutions he revised his lessons. During the time allotted for reading story books he noted in his diary, along with other sundry matters, "Great is the discoverer of zero". Then, picking up a sheet of paper and a pen, he sat down to compose an article for the school magazine.

# RAIN CYCLE

*Translated from "Brustichakra"*

Banka was initiated into Bollywood lore by Chiku bhai, the neighbourhood gossip. It was he who told them that black clothes were a strict no-no for film hero Dev Anand. He had explained why. Wearing a black shirt and trousers, and dark glasses, Dev Anand was one day driving his black car in Bombay, and hundreds of girls jumped to death from their rooftops, Chiku bhai said. Likewise, the colour movie "Daag", he said, was in reality about the personal life of superhero Rajesh Khanna. Rakhi was like his wife and Sharmila Tagore was his lover. When in real life both of them fought over Rajesh Khanna, he married none of them. Instead, he tied the knot with Dimple Kapadia who was much younger in age. When Rajesh was the one asking, who could decline?

Sometimes Nani doubted Chiku bhai. She asked, "Hundreds of girls?"

"Wouldn't hundreds have died? All of them were leaning out of their balconies and watching Dev Anand. After ten to fifteen had jumped, the police picked up Dev

Anand and took him to the police station. They fitted him out in multicoloured dresses and sent him home. They also asked him never to roam around the streets of Bombay dressed in black. However great a person may be, they have to be afraid of the police, don't they? Police is the most powerful of all. And Bombay Police! Oh my god! Even the mightiest have to salute the Bombay Police."

While talking about the police, Chiku bhai's voice was so grave that Banka and the others would be gripped by an unknown fear. Nobody knew whether Nani believed in his words or not, but she never extended the argument. Chiku bhai was very touchy. If somebody contradicted him, he would completely turn his back on them, deigning neither to see nor speak to them.

Once, Gagan, the other emerging gossip, was sitting on their veranda when Chiku bhai turned up. Banka and the others sat in a circle around Gagan. He was telling them about his school. How big their school was, how brilliant the teachers were, how a meal was served to all the students during lunch time, how there was school inspection every month, how the headmaster of their school was addressed as the Principal, how a Principal was greater than a headmaster, how their Principal surreptitiously kept watch on the way teachers were teaching in the class, and how if any teacher made a mistake while teaching, they were sacked on the spot and so on. They were listening to Gagan so attentively that they had not noticed Chiku bhai's arrival. Chiku bhai observed the scene for a few seconds and slunk away, and didn't return for a month. He had watched four films during that time. Banka could not take it anymore. One day he decided to take the bull by the horns, "Chiku bhai, you do not come over anymore?"

Chiku bhai answered, "Why, you have your Gagan, he will tell you stories. What value do I have for you?"

"Has Gagan ever watched a film that he will tell us stories?" Banka protested. "He is so poor. He will talk only about school, his teachers, his studies. He gives himself such airs because he studies well." Banka gave a little spin to the facts.

That did the trick. Chiku bhai started visiting them again, as usual, after Banka's tutor left. There was no restriction at home on Chiku bhai's visits. For one thing, his family were their immediate neighbours. And secondly, they were rich enough to make one's eyes pop out of their sockets. His family had telephones and cars at home. Sometimes even Chacha used their phone to talk with God knows whom. The most important thing about them was, they watched movies every week. They often took Mother along, but Mother never took Banka and the other children with her. Her logic was that if you went to the movies you would go astray; you would not be able to do well in studies. Banka never pleaded to go to movies out of fear of Father and Chacha, but Nani had once wanted to go.

Mother sternly warned her, "If you are so very keen to watch movies, I will marry you off to a rickshaw puller from Andhra Pradesh, so that you can watch movies to your heart's content. Give me your books and school bag. Let me burn them."

Nobody at home raised the issue of movies after that. Fortunately, Chiku bhai narrated the stories after watching the movies. After the tutor left, Chiku bhai managed to slip away until dinner time. Every evening it was either meat or fish at Chiku bhai's home. Chiku bhai would arrive, sniffing his fingers. He also let Banka sniff them before sitting down to narrate the stories of the movies he had watched. Nani and Banka would be waiting desperately for the lowdown on the new movie. Even Chhotu, whether he understood or not, would be all ears, leaning on Nani for Chiku bhai's words. Chiku bhai would talk about Raj Kapoor, Rajesh Khanna, Pran: how both Pran and Sanjay Khan set out for Bombay together to become heroes in movies; the director of the film handed over two swords to them and asked them to fight. Sanjay Khan won the sword fight and became a hero without knowing "a b c" of acting while Pran had to settle for a villain's role. Pran was so good at acting that when he came on screen shoe sales in the town shot up; while watching the movie the audience threw their shoes at the screen version of Pran and the next day they had to buy new shoes for themselves. For this reason, the shoe-sellers collected money and bought shoes for Pran's entire family. As for Pran's family, did they ever buy shoes for themselves? Never.

During those moments Banka wondered how much

Chiku bhai knew. When he grew up he would definitely watch films. He would know about Dev Anand, Pran and others. He would tell his friends the stories of movies, the way Chiku bhai was telling. But it seemed he was losing his earlier enthusiasm for those stories of late. This seemed to coincide with his leaving Cuttack and coming to Choudwar, his father's place of work. Immediately after the move his enthusiasm was undiminished. He had watched several movies with his new friend Abhijeet bhai at the Officers' Club. Movies featuring Pran, Dev Anand, Dilip Kumar, Rajesh Khanna, Amitabh Bachchan. Abhijeet bhai's father used to pick them up after school for film shows at his club. Since Abhijeet bhai's father was a senior officer, Banka's parents were not able to say no. But after watching a few films Banka lost interest in them, even in the ones showing the black-dress-wearing Dev Anand. What did the girls see in this man to make them jump from their roofs? Banka could never come to terms with the idea of dying by jumping from the roof because of someone's appearance. Perhaps those were Chiku bhai's cock and bull stories. But to tell the truth, Chiku bhai's stories were more endearing than the real experience of watching movies. He remembered how he remained awake in bed till midnight, reflecting upon Chiku bhai's stories. How fervently he had prayed to Hanuman! "Oh! Bajrangbali, make me rich too. Let us eat fish, meat and egg curry every day. Let there be a telephone in our house too. Let Father and Mother turn into good human beings and allow us to visit cinema halls."

Although a tad belated, the simian god had finally granted this prayer. The first intimations of that came from Mother. Mother, who went about performing the household chores with a face hung like a blackened earthenware pot all the time, was sparkling with joy that day. She was feeding the children more than their fair share. Her happiness was palpable; Grandma, Chachi, Chacha and even the youngest Chacha were getting proportionately more and more wearied. Their faces had started drooping lower and lower. At bedtime, Mother disclosed the secret, "We won't stay here anymore."

Banka asked, "Where will we go?"

"To Father's workplace," Mother answered.

Since Grandma pampered Nani a lot, she was Nani's favourite person. She protested, "No, Mother, it is nice here. Grandma is here, Grandpa is here, Chacha is here. We won't go anywhere else."

Banka felt the same way. As it is, Father was so irritable when he came home on the weekend. He was always enquiring about their progress in studies. If they went to stay at his workplace the skin on his back would be pulverised by regular beating. But he did not say anything openly.

Mother said, "We will have such huge quarters to stay in there. You will have separate rooms for studying. Now you are all grown up. You have to focus more on your studies."

Then snarling at God-knows-whom, she spewed her venom. "I have driven myself to death slaving for this idle family. If my children turn out to be uneducated fools will anyone have their back?"

Much later Banka came to know that Mother had been after Father for a long time for this move to Choudwar. But he had not agreed. Then Mother had unleashed her ultimate weapon. She said: "All my time is taken up in the kitchen of this crowded house. There is no one to supervise the children's studies. If this continues, the children will turn into wastrels."

Grandma and the others were not in favour of the shift; but who had the guts to contradict Father? At last, the day of parting arrived. Grandma had already left for her village with Grandpa. The elder Chacha went out on a tour with Chachi. Only San Chacha was around to pack the belongings and see them off. After Father left with the truck loaded with their belongings, Chacha came with them to the bus stop. Even though he had beaten him up several times, when Banka bade him goodbye before boarding the bus with Mother, his eyes became moist with tears. In fact, Banka had been feeling like crying for the last three days. Their friends and neighbours invited them for meals at their houses when they came to know that they were moving. Banka felt overwhelming grief while having a meal especially at Chiku bhai's and Pramila's places. Suppressing his tears, Banka told Chiku bhai, "I will study at a good school. Much bigger than ours. The headmaster of that school has won the President's medal."

Chiku bhai sulked, "You will definitely forget us

Banka. Yes, it is so natural for you to do so. Who are we for you?" He ran away from there lest his tears got the better of him. The same scene was repeated at Pramila's place. Although she maintained some distance, her elder sisters surrounded him. They asked, "Banka, are you leaving us all for good? But you don't seem to be sad? You don't have a heart it seems."

Banka boasted, "We have a phone connection in the house there. We will go to school by an office vehicle." He spoke in a loud voice so that Pramila could easily hear. Although she was pretending not to listen, Banka was confident that Pramila was all ears. But for some reason Pramila was not teary-eyed. During their enactment of Ramlila, of course, this fair-skinned Pramila, who played Sita, used to shed copious tears in the Sita-abduction scene. And since Banka was dark, the elder sisters decked him out in the role of Rama. In the scene where Sita was supposed to sit beside Rama, Pramila came and sat close to him, but whispered in his ears, "Who is he to me? Why should I sit near him?"

Banka enjoyed Pramila's tears, her manner of sitting close to him and her whispered banter immensely. He thought Pramila was saying all this to him in jest, for deep inside she loved him very much. In any case girls were by nature fond of acting. But even when she heard about Banka leaving the place for good, there was no trace of tears in her eyes. He was confused. When he bade goodbye to Chacha at the bus stop all his confusions and repressed emotions found an outlet in the form of waves of sobs which prompted his mother to comment, "You are now a grown-up boy, why are you crying? You can come to Cuttack anytime during vacations."

Banka had not understood the meaning of growing up then. He had thought only girls grew up. When Pramila had grown up, her mother had invited eight boys like him to a feast at her home. After the feast Pramila herself served them kheer. Tears were streaming from her eyes while she served them. Her mother was prompting her from behind, "O dear, why are you crying? Is it nice to cry while serving food to friends? They are mere kids, you are a grown girl. You should not be shy before them."

Banka had understood then that only girls grew up. Though Pramila was younger than him in age, she had grown up and was serving kheer to them. It was only later that he came to know how boys grow up. In a few days he would be studying at a college in Cuttack. He would leave the large official quarters, telephone, office car, Abhijeet bhai, cinema-watching at the club, the school, and the President's award-winning Principal behind. These things, of course, were not exciting for him anymore. The things that appeared to be beyond his reach in Cuttack were easily accessible here. But then they appeared very ordinary to him now.

Perhaps there was something off somewhere. He felt as if he did not desire what he could get with ease. And he did not know what he desired. The same was also true of Father and Mother. At Cuttack Mother was secretly disgusted with Grandma, Chacha and Chachi. She told them many pleasures were awaiting them at Father's workplace. Now at Choudwar she would get irritated with Father and her own children, including Banka. She would hold Father responsible for having neglected her health for a long time. Of course, sometimes when she was in a good mood she would cuddle Banka and express her hope that all her suffering would come to an end once Banka grew up and took up a highly-paid job.

Did growing up mean this perpetual discontentment with the present, obsessing over the future and pining for the past? Perhaps some people were fated to be like this. Banka saw other adults around him who never had any doubt about how they lived their lives. Like Abhijeet bhai's father. He was happy with his job, his car, his phone, his club, his library and his house parties. Why was Banka's fate like this? To look for reasons behind every event, to get into a quandary while looking for reasons, to overlook the pleasures at hand and be immersed in confusion and then, after letting go of all pleasures, sinking into a deep sorrow. The way Banka was now.

Sudden rain interrupted Banka's thoughts. The boys who had accompanied him to the playground left for their homes. But Banka kept sitting on a wayside culvert near the playground. He was mentally shuffling unsolvable questions, turning memories from the past around in his mind. *What was so tempting about growing up?* Banka thought to himself. His childhood in Cuttack had been much better. Chiku bhai's stories, Pramila's acting, her snide remarks. Those stories might have been false,

Pramila's acting might have been put on, but his own faith and joy were pure. Credulous childhood was far better than this confused grown-upness. But how could anyone return to his childhood.

Drops of rain had started falling. Should he run down to Mishra Uncle's quarters, which were close to the playground, and wait for the rain to stop? Or should he make his way back home and get soaked? Of course, Mother would be angry if he got drenched. She would chide him for not thinking about the upcoming examination and inviting a fever. Banka was unable to decide. Meanwhile the rain had started gathering force. It was now coming down in cascades. But Banka kept sitting on the culvert holding his cricket bat. It was already dusk. Now he was slowly starting to enjoy the rain. The rain seemed to be washing away all his confusion. He remembered the lesson, the rain cycle, taught in his Geography class. During summer the water from the seas, the rivers and even drains evaporated. The vapour formed clouds and came back as water to the rivers, streams and the seas during the rainy season. Banka smiled a little on remembering this. Then without worrying about Mother's reprimand he returned home like a jay-walker, getting a thorough soaking.

# THE ACCOUNT OF A PILGRIMAGE

*Translated from "Jatrara Dinalipi"*

The door opened to reveal Debashis. Clad in a pair of trousers, well-shod and with a pair of sunglasses perched across his eyes. A watch was wrapped around his right wrist, the way the Mathematics teacher wears it. The shock of hair on his head was cut in a wavy style currently in fashion.

Banka kept staring at him, stunned.

"Don't you recognise me?" Debashis asked.

Before Banka could answer, Mother's voice was heard from inside: "Who is at the door?"

"Ma, Debashis...?" Mother rushed out from the kitchen, her palms still smeared with blackgram paste.

"Did you travel alone all the way from Cuttack? Do your parents know? How is your mother?" she went on.

Debashis did not answer any of her questions. He just kept smiling, the way kings do in yatras. Her questions irritated Banka. Just because she had her children under her wing, she probably thought everyone was like her, out to tie their children to their pallus. She never allowed her children to take a step outside the house. If you went to the playground you had to come back before six o'clock. Outings were limited to either maternal or paternal grandparents' village homes. That too, under her own personal supervision. Banka felt a sense of disquiet when he read the adventurous stories of Huck Finn and Tom Sawyer, sitting at the library. Despite being orphans, their fate seemed so alluring. The huge Mississippi river, rafts, guns, hidden treasures flashed across his mind's eye.

Mother served them both dosas. He loved dosas. But after seeing Debashis, he had lost his taste for food. Forget Huck and Tom, even this Debashis was so lucky. Wearing shoes and socks, sporting the latest hair-style, he had travelled all the way from Cuttack to Choudwar, alone. He must have visited many other places as well. As a student, he was not as good as Banka. His father too was a low-paid government employee, much below Banka's father's rank. But Mother would always tell him to study well. If you are a good student you will be able to travel widely, she would say. So Banka would return home before evening set in. Say his daily prayer. On vacations he would be allowed to go as far as the Officers' Library. Of course, he loved reading the World Literature series that the library stocked, but sometimes he, like other boys, felt like taking a trip to the cashew-nut forest near the air-field close to their quarters. Collect cashew-nut seeds, visit cinema houses at Cuttack. But to these, Mother would always say an emphatic "no".

"Why don't you eat?" Mother asked as she tipped another dosa onto his plate. Debashis had, by that time, polished off two dosas, and was on a third one. Mother would start blabbering unnecessarily if he said he did not have an appetite, so he quickly pushed the dosa down his gullet, drank a glass of water to wash it down, belched loudly and got up, picking up his own plate. This was one of Father's rules. One had to clean one's plate after meals. Sometimes Banka broke this rule. But after seeing Debashis, he felt like demonstrating that he was an obedient boy. He was meeting Debashis after two and a half years. He seemed to have changed a lot in that time. His speech, gait, smile, and deportment had started resembling those of an adult. But Banka himself was where he had always been.

Will the boys become like Debashis after the matriculation examination? That did not seem reasonable. Hardly a couple of days had passed since the examination ended. Did Debashis change so drastically in just a couple of days? Maybe cities like Cuttack bring about such change. Boys must change so rapidly there. He got terribly upset with Mother. Because of her insistence they had to shift to Choudwar where his father was posted. How wonderful those days were! Father would come to Cuttack only on Saturday evenings. On Sunday evenings they would listen to radio plays or cricket commentary together. He never got angry with them. Now that they were living together he would lose his temper over trifles. One was rebuked for playing past the designated time, for stealthily reading journals. Moreover, the place was rather sleepy. There was no market, no roadside paan-shops, almost nothing. Had they been in Cuttack, maybe they would have bought him full pants and goggles. Like Debashis he would have gone to school wearing shoes.

After breakfast they were sitting in Banka's study-room on the roof-top, it was relatively isolated from the rest of the house. There was no fear of getting disturbed by his sister or younger brother. Banka suddenly picked up Debashis's sunglasses and held them before his eyes. Oh! How colourful the world looked! The ferocity of the sun's rays was subdued. There was a bluish tinge to everything he saw. Debashis lay stretched on the bed. He suddenly sat up and exclaimed.

"Don't, don't look through that. You may harm your eyes!"

Banka got scared. "How come your eyes are intact," he asked hesitantly.

"I am used to it," Debashis answered. "Once you begin wearing them, you have to use them regularly. Don't you see, I have to wear them whenever I go out in the sun? This is a dangerous habit. We are already spoiled. You are a good boy, why should you take a risk? You have a bright future ahead of you."

Banka did not trust his explanation. Nonetheless he put the sunglasses down on the bed. He felt Debashis was talking about some other form of spoiling. The sunglasses might be indirectly linked with that. Slowly Debashis was turning into a bundle of mysteries. He wanted to ask him how he had spent the last one and a half years. What the other boys of his class in his old school were doing. How Debashis's parents were getting on. Whether his former teachers remembered him. But these questions might sound very childish to Debashis, he reckoned. When they studied in the school at Cuttack, Debashis was his best friend, even though he was a backbencher, not good at studies, and afraid of the teachers. If he failed to work out his sums, he got them done by Banka early in the morning before school hours and only then was he able to face the teachers. He was always so obsequious towards Banka that their classmates teased him by calling him Banka's lackey. Now Debashis seemed to be full of confidence, and Banka felt like cowering before him.

"Would you like to have a smoke?" Debashis brought out a packet of cigarettes from his pocket and held it towards Banka.

"No, no, Mother will kill me if she came to know. About my father, the less said, the better," Banka responded, terrified. Not that he had not smoked bidis a couple of times, prodded by his naughty friends, but this was always outside the ambit of home. Whenever he had smoked during lunch-breaks at school he had almost choked on his coughs and sneezes. He had to suck peppermint candies before entering the classroom.

Still lying on the bed, Debashis smoked his cigarette, inhaling the smoke and releasing it in small ringlets, like Dev Anand, the film hero. He gave the impression that the bed, the house, Banka's entire family, even the whole world was under his sway.

"Please put it out now. We can smoke later. If Mother comes up she will be able to smell it." Although he felt ashamed about saying this, Banka had no choice.

Debashis smiled, as usual, beaming with self-confidence, and brought out a small vial of cheap Kanta scent. Opening the cap he touched the mouth of the vial to Banka's shirt collar. The smell of the scent intermixed with that of the smoke of Capstan cigarettes wafted in the room, aided by the air from the table-fan.

Banka felt as if the solution to life's every problem lay within Debashis's grasp.

"Let's go to Puri," Debashis suggested suddenly. "Puri?" Banka was taken unawares. "Have you been there earlier?" This time Debashis broke into loud laughter.

"I must visit Puri at least once a month, for the taste of 'green', I mean the green paste of bhang. There is a local club near Uncle's house. Uncle's son practises wrestling there. He prepares wonderful bhang sherbet, mixing it with cashew nut paste and 'rabri'. If you taste it once you will feel like staying there forever."

"You are one lucky guy," Now Banka had to admit openly. The little pride he took in being a good student, in his father's higher position, and in his own disciplined life, melted away at once. He felt relieved. Once he acknowledged Debashis's obvious superiority in his own mind, he was able to get on with him easily. He had been unable to so far because of his inability to accept this truth. Was what Father, Mother, Nani and his uncles told him false all along? What was the point of only reading about either Tom or Huck or Tarzan or Jim Hawkins of *Treasure Island* if you could not live a life like theirs? His life had been meaningless so far. Debashis at least had been living an adventurous life in his own fashion.

"I feel a strong desire to visit Puri with you," Banka pleaded the way his next-door neighbour Baliar Singh Uncle's dog wagged its tail in front of him.

"Come along. When did I deny you?" Debashis answered with gravitas worthy of an adult.

"Will Mother allow?" Banka's voice sounded pathetic.

But Debashis's voice was unperturbed as usual. "Why should you ask about Puri?"

"What do you mean?" Banka was unable to understand.

"We will tell her that we are going to Cuttack, to our house. To celebrate my birthday. You will come back after the celebration."

Banka was unable to muster up the courage to tell such a lie. Every evening they prayed,

> Why should I be afraid to tell the truth?
> I will tell the truth even at the cost of my life.

Moreover, what if somebody saw him in Puri? If he chanced upon Chacha or any other acquaintance on the way or at the railway station? Chacha would start thrashing him right away. And if the matter reached Father's ears then all hell would break loose.

"I can't do this. Try if you can."

That evening at dinner Debashis came to the point directly. "Auntie, I had in fact come to take Banka along to Cuttack. The 'Pala' and the related religious rituals are going to be performed on the occasion of my sixteenth birthday. Banka should come with me tomorrow. He will stay at our house for a couple of days after the ceremony. Banka is such a good student. He will definitely get into Ravenshaw College. During his stay in our house I will acquaint him with the college, hostels and the office building. If he knows the place beforehand, it will be helpful when he starts going there."

Father sat not far away, reading the newspaper. Drawn by Debashis's guardian-like talk, he raised his eyes from the newspaper and looked at the boys. Banka was scared. Nobody dared to be chatty in front of Father. He was reserved by nature, and if he got angry on hearing such cunning talk, then the matter would end there. Banka looked at his father from the corner of his eyes. No, there was no trace of anger; rather there was a faint glimmer of a smile on his usually grave face. Banka felt assured.

Mother, on the other hand, seemed to fall from the sky at Debashis's words. "No, no, how can he go with you like this? He has never gone away from home on his own. Moreover, he has health issues. His father will not permit it."

Mother's last remark was fated to fail, for Father immediately responded, "Let him go if he so desires. He will get smart if he goes out. He will meet people. At some point he has to go it alone. Let him get used to it." Father went back to the world of his newspaper after this pronouncement.

Stopped in her tracks, Mother only sulked, "Let him do whatever he wants. How would it bother me? But do not drag me into it if anything untoward happens."

Though irked by Mother's words, Banka kept quiet so as not to aggravate the situation. Father had agreed so easily; now if he created a scene, things might get out of hand. After getting the go-ahead from Father, Banka went and quietly packed his clothes, toothbrush, paste, etc., in a bag, ignoring his sulking mother. His brother and sister were burning with envy, but who had the guts to override Father's diktat? Although outwardly grave, Banka was overflowing with joy. He was unable to sleep properly thinking when night would give way to morning and they would set out for Cuttack. It was true he had seen a bit of Cuttack; but things there must have changed, the way Debashis had changed. There must be huge posters of stars like Rajesh Khanna, Dev Anand or Hema Malini in front of the movie halls, Prabhat, Capital and Hind. Although he had never had the good fortune of watching a Hindi film inside a movie hall, what great joy he had derived looking at the hoardings in front of the cinema houses when he was studying at Cuttack! He had no idea how far into the night he had marched imagining his face next to the faces of various film heroines. Finally, he had taken a vow that when he grew up he would go to Bombay and become a film hero. His posters would also be plastered across cinema halls at Cuttack. Only then Mother would come to realise his worth. Even Debashis, who was showing off in a pair of sunglasses, would come to his senses. He would stand in a queue to watch his film, but tickets would be sold out. He would beg for a ticket in front of black-marketeers like Chheta. But what if Debashis went to Bombay? What if he too became a film hero? With his handsome face, he might be preferred over Banka. With a lot of trepidation he asked Debashis next to him, "What will you be, when you grow up?"

"Shut up and go to sleep quickly. If we miss the first steamer in the morning, we will not be able to catch the train to Puri," Debashis snapped in a sleepy, hoarse voice, before turning on his side and falling back into sleep. Now Banka lost himself in thoughts of the impending visit to Puri. What would Puri look like? Early in his childhood they had gone to Konark once. It was winter. Shivering in the cold, they had watched the sunrise at Chandrabhaga. He had heard that the sun jumps into the sky from the depths of the sea. In a half-awakened state Banka could not, however, catch any such sight on the foggy horizon. He had never had the opportunity to visit Puri. While he drew images in his mind of the temple of Lord Jagannath, the unique kind of meals served in earthenware pots, the sea like a vast swimming pool, visitors from all over the country and abroad, the servitors of the temple with elephantiasis, the temple of Bata Mangala, the Atharanala Bridge near the entrance to the town, the famous Narendra Pond in which Lord Jagannath reportedly has His annual boat-ride, despite himself he was overtaken by sleep.

"Wake up, bloody fool. I have taken my bath already

and this idiot is still snoring loudly." Banka woke up at Debashis's yelling and saw that he was actually all dressed and ready to go. Banka finished his morning ablutions and got ready in no time. He put a couple of old copies of *Jahnamamu*, the popular children's journal, and the book *Uncle Tom's Cabin*, which he was halfway through, in his bag and got ready. When he touched Mother's feet by way of farewell she gave him some pocket money and said, "Keep the money safely. Do not lose it. You are a careless fool. Why are you so eager to step out of home at the first chance?"

Banka ignored his mother's words. They sent back his father's peon who had come to see them off at the bus stop. Then they proceeded towards the steamer jetty instead. The first steam-boat towards Jobra was on the verge of leaving, and they hurriedly boarded the boat.

After blowing a long horn the steamer moved ahead. It was Banka's first boat-ride. From the moment Debashis had proposed the steamer-ride Banka had given free rein to his imagination. He had felt excited, remembering Huck and Jim's adventurous journey across the Mississippi. At the same time he was scared when he recounted the dangers they encountered on the way. He felt his heart pound on remembering the episode of the steamboat hitting Huck's raft. Fortunately, Banka was on a steamboat and not on a raft. Even then...

Suddenly the steamer started swaying like the pendulum of a clock while cruising through the unfathomable waters of the Mahanadi. Banka's heart skipped a beat. What if water enters the boat while it sways? According to the sutra of Archimedes, if the weight of an object is greater than the weight of the volume of water it displaces then the object will sink. What if the boat really sank? Or if there was a hole somewhere through which water forced its way in? The banks of the river were not visible to Banka at this point. What would he do in the middle of the river? He looked at Debashis. Legs spread like one poised to take on his adversary in a wrestling bout, Debashis was standing courageously in the aisle of the steam-boat when most of the adult passengers were seated on the benches. Resting his palms on his hips he was looking up towards the horizon.

"Do you know how to swim?" Banka asked, moving closer to Debashis.

"Bloody fool, haven't you watched us swimming across the river to the island over there to fetch berries? You have a habit of hiding inside the house. Haven't I asked you several times to come along? Your mother never permitted you. Have you not learnt how to swim?"

"No. When would I get the opportunity? There is a swimming pool at our Officers' Club, but the water there is only up to the waist. Not deep like the river. How deep is the water here?" Banka was almost in tears.

"Some forty to fifty feet."

"Which is easier for swimming, less or more water?"

"Once you learn swimming it makes no difference. One can swim irrespective of the depth of the water."

"Oh, is that so? Another thing. Can you swim holding two or three persons?"

"Are you a bloated fool or what? How can I swim holding a couple of people? Haven't you learnt anything in the Boy Scout classes? Like the methods of rescuing a drowning man? One should not go anywhere near the person. One has to throw one end of a towel towards him, which he will clasp, and you can then drag him, holding the other end. Or carefully push him from behind towards safety."

"Yes, yes, I know those lessons very well. I was just asking you. In fact, I was testing how strong and courageous you are." To be honest, Banka did not want to talk further on the subject. Because, although he was asking all his questions in a whisper, Debashis was answering in a loud voice, flaunting his superior knowledge. Other passengers had started lapping up their conversation. Banka did not want to let on before total strangers that he was terrified. He desperately wanted to change the subject. Fortunately, they could now see the shore at a distance. Probably, it was Cuttack. But how was it that the shore looked like a jungle full of large and small shrubs? Where was the famous Jobra Pole near the jetty that can be seen from afar?

"Have we arrived at Cuttack?" Banka asked.

"This is a riverine island. How can Cuttack come so quickly?"

Banka never knew there was such a huge island within the Mahanadi. He was amused that here too there was a riverine island like Jackson Island from *The Adventures of Huckleberry Finn*. The only difference between the book and his own experience was that he was so afraid because, unlike Huck, he did not know how to swim. Although of the same age, Huck was much more courageous than him. Debashis, of course, was equally daring. He was on his feet confidently throughout the entire journey. He silently cursed his own parents to his heart's content. They were responsible for turning him into a coward. Had he tried from childhood he could have learnt how to swim. He could also have roamed around alone wherever he wanted. He would not have had to constantly worry about getting a job after studying well; would not have wasted all his time poring over books.

"After this there is a stopover at T.P.M. After passengers board there, it will head towards Jobra," Debashis added.

True to his words the steam boat approached the jetty at T.P.M. in a while. Banka got a new lease on life after seeing land. Some passengers got off there while a few others came onboard the steamer. Banka had read about this T.P.M., Titagarh Paper Mill, in his geography book. After seeing the place with his own eyes he was overcome with a sense of exhilaration. The fear he had felt earlier when they were in water evaporated gradually. One gentleman who had boarded the steamer at T.P.M. sat down near him and asked, "Are you a student?"

"Yes, I have given the matriculation examination" Banka answered.

"Where are you going?"

"Puri," he blurted out the truth involuntarily. There was no way of taking it back.

"Good, good. It is good to go for Lord Jagannath's blessings after the exam. What will you be when you grow up?"

"When I grow up...?" Banka could not make sense of the question instantly.

"I mean what is your aim in life?" The gentleman tried to explain.

Many a time the teachers of his class had asked him to compose an essay on the topic "My Aim in Life". Sometimes he wrote of becoming an IAS officer, and at other times a doctor or an engineer. But those essays were written to get good marks in the test. Now, this gentleman was asking a real question. Banka could not figure out what to answer. Life certainly did not mean some kind of a job! Did those who did not have good jobs not have a life; were they not human beings? Would his life be finished after his job ended?

"When he grows up, he will join the army. I will become an IPS officer," Debashis answered and saved him from a crisis. Banka realised that Debashis was mocking the gentleman, but he could not detect the mockery. He said, "Good, good, the country needs such patriots."

As soon as the steamer docked at the Jobra jetty, Debashis almost dragged him out and they climbed into a hand-drawn rickshaw. "Let us hurry. It is already time for the departure of the fast passenger train. If we miss it we will not be able to return from Puri tonight."

They headed straight towards the Cuttack railway

station. A couple of minutes after they had booked tickets the train arrived. There was not much of a rush, probably because it was a Sunday. They occupied two seats near the window.

It was as if someone had smeared a magic ointment in Banka's eyes. He was experiencing many things for the first time in his life. First a trip on a motor-boat, then a train ride, that too unaccompanied by an adult. He vowed to remember the names of all the stations where the train halted on its way. He would count all the trees, ponds and rivers. But shortly after the train started moving, he felt sleepy. By nature, he was rather lazy and, on top of it, Debashis had woken him up very early in the morning. When the soft morning breeze of early April tickled him through the open window he plunged into a deep slumber.

"Get up. We have reached. Bloody fellow slept all the way from Cuttack to Puri like someone intoxicated on bhang."

Banka woke up with a start. For a few moments he could not figure out where he was. Wiping away the saliva that had trickled from his mouth and the drops of sweat from his face he followed Debashis, clutching his bag. There was bright sunlight outside. The air bore the heat of a mid-April day. The dream of his first time away from home had so overwhelmed him that he had not been able to relish his breakfast properly, and he had left after eating very little. Now the pangs of hunger were multiplied by the promise of feasting on abhada—the sacramental food—in the temple premises.

As they boarded, Debashis told the rickshaw-puller, "Take us to Chitrakar Sahi." Banka was confused by Debashis's instruction.

"I am hungry," he pleaded.

"We will eat there."

"But we were supposed to eat the sacramental food, at Anand Bazar in the temple precincts," Banka protested mildly. A lovely picture of Anand Bazar was etched in his mind, since he had heard the devotional songs of the famous Muslim poet Salabega, which his elder sister sang during her music lessons.

"What a fool you are! Abhada will be available only after 2:30 pm. Our train for the return journey is at 3 o'clock. Will we catch it if we wait for it? If we miss that train we cannot return to Cuttack tonight."

Banka could not understand. He had reckoned that they would stay at Debashis's uncle's place for a couple of days. They would sample the famous bhang sharbat, the intoxicating drink, which his uncle's son prepared. They would enjoy various other pleasures peculiar to Puri, whose tantalising picture Debashis had painted, and then they would return. But now he was given to understand that they would return the same day. After paying the rickshaw puller they entered a thatched house. Probably some sort of restaurant. A middle-aged woman laid two mats on the floor and served some rice, dalma—a lentil dish with various vegetables—and sour chutney on two banana leaves. Banka was really hungry, and the food tasted divine. He ate a large quantity and drank some water to wash it down. After Debashis paid for the meal, they came out and walked some distance before entering another hut. There were several statues made up of clay, wood and stone arranged in an outer room. A bald artisan was polishing a statue with some oily substance in a corner.

"Uncle, do you have a statue of the divine couple Radha and Krishna?" asked Debashis.

From the crowd of statues assembled there, the man picked up a wonderful statue of Radha and Krishna. As he held it up, Debashis asked, "How much?"

"One hundred and fifty rupees."

After haggling over the price for a long time the man agreed to sell it for a hundred rupees. "Lend me fifty rupees," Debashis asked. Without a demur Banka handed him a fifty rupee note. Debashis placed the statue in Banka's bag. Coming out of the hut, Debashis made him walk a long distance before hiring a rickshaw. "To the station," he instructed. Completely confused, Banka tagged along.

Upon reaching the railway station they looked at the huge clock hanging from a beam in the platform. It was 2:30 in the afternoon. Half an hour still, for the train to depart. Now Banka could not restrain himself any more.

"The temple and the sea....?" He managed to blurt out, his voice cracked in grief.

"Can you visit the temple within half an hour? And will you go to the beach in this blazing sun? Won't we come here again when you get admission in Cuttack? We will visit the temple then, to our heart's content. We will bathe in the sea. My cousin is an expert in tackling the sea waves," Debashis assured him.

Banka wanted to ask why then they had come to Puri at all. Would it not have been better to watch a matinee show at Hind Cinema than going to Puri in name only and missing out on everything Puri had to offer? Now that Debashis had taken all the money his mother had given him he would not be able to watch a movie even if he wanted.

"Give me twenty rupees. Let me buy the tickets. If there is a crowd we may have to stand in the queue," Debashis suggested.

"You have already taken all the money my mother gave me,' Banka clarified.

"Okay, don't worry. We will travel W.T."

Debashis explained to an uncomprehending Banka that W.T. meant travelling Without Ticket.

"But what if the police catch us?" Banka was scared.

"Not police, you fool, T.T.E., Train Ticket Examiner. Nothing will happen. Why are you getting scared? Living in Choudwar has turned you into an incorrigible coward," Debashis teased him.

Debashis removed the full pants, sunglasses and the wrist watch he was wearing and placed them in Banka's bag. He was wearing a pair of underpants underneath. Now, both of them looked like two young boys. But the socks and full shoes Debashis was wearing didn't go with his underpants.

"Listen, today is Pramila's birthday. A few days ago she told me that she likes the statues of Radha and Krishna, the kind that are made at Puri. One of her aunts had got one from here. I thought I will give her one as a gift today," Debashis explained the real purpose of the Puri trip.

"Which Pramila?"

"The one who lives on our block, the daughter of Chandrakanta Uncle. She played with us, do you remember? I love her."

Banka felt as if someone had hit him in the head with a hammer. Banka had not forgotten Pramila. As children they had acted in the Ramlila, imitating the performance staged every summer at the municipality grounds. Pramila was fair like a champak flower, and played the role of Sita. Although he did not have a single quality of Lord Ramachandra, Banka was allowed to play that role because of the dark colour of his skin. His lackey Debashis gratefully accepted the role of Hanuman, the greatest devotee of the Lord. But, here, in a matter of two years, this Debashis had graduated to Pramila's lover! He must be lying, Banka thought. Pramila can't love this rapscallion. He is a good-looking good-for-nothing. Would a girl like Pramila love this idiot just because he was good looking? He was not a good student. A pompous snob, rather. Pramila, after all, was a good student. It was doubtful whether the wretch would be able to pass the matriculation examination. A little while ago he was boasting he would become an IPS officer when he grew up. Forget IPS, he would end up as a constable.

Banka was terribly disgusted with Debashis. He felt like deserting him then and there and running away. But where could he go? He was clueless about roads and directions. Moreover, there was no money in his pocket. If Debashis did not lend him some money in Cuttack, his return home to Choudwar would be in jeopardy.

As the train reached the platform, Banka climbed into a compartment with a great deal of hesitation. Debashis instructed him on how to get off the train at every station; how to board a compartment other than the one the T.T.E. was in; how to slip into a bathroom if by chance you came face to face with the T.T.E. and so on. Banka detested this cat and mouse game. On the other hand, the fear of going to jail for travelling without ticket made his heart beat rapidly. But what was the alternative? In the process of getting off the train at one station and re-boarding it at another one of his slippers accidently fell off. The train had started moving by then. Before he could figure out what to do Debashis pulled away the other slipper and threw it out with great force.

"What will you do with one piece? Rather, someone who finds both will be able to use them," Debashis explained.

Banka was deaf to his words. He was thoroughly disenchanted. What kind of freedom was this? Now they were running around like petty thieves. He had heard from someone that in jail, hardened adult criminals forced younger criminals to massage their hands and feet. If they felt like it they also did bad things with the younger criminals. These thoughts now disturbed him terribly. He began cursing Debashis silently. When he was tired of cursing he started reciting the Hanuman Chalisa speedily. 'O Lord, Bajrangbali, please save me from this danger. I have committed a great sin. It was a big mistake to lie in order to go on this cursed trip. Please forgive me. At least for once, save me from this grave danger."

At Khurda Road Junction they got down from the train, but Banka was unable to walk barefoot on the hot platform. Debashis took his bag from him and said, "You do one thing. You get into a toilet in the compartment and stay put. At Cuttack you get down. I will let you know when we reach there."

Banka hated getting inside the toilet with bare feet. But out of compulsion he entered a toilet and locked it from inside. He tried to hold his breath to avoid the foul smell, but for how long could one hold their breath? He inhaled some fresh air through the window of the bathroom and held it for as long as he could. After releasing the breath he repeated the process. While performing this repetitive act he lost track of how far the train had travelled, where Debashis was at that point, or how long it would take to reach Cuttack. After some time, he decided to wash the toilet clean by collecting water in his palms from the tap. At regular intervals there were knocks on the door from outside. But Banka was oblivious to them. Once the stink subsided somewhat, he paused to read the vulgar comments and indecent drawings etched on the walls.

Who drew such vulgar pictures and wrote such obscene comments? What pleasure did they derive from it? Boys like Debashis must have written them. Before passing matriculation examination he had started falling in love. Did people feel like indulging in such vulgarity when they were in love?

The train stopped after blowing a long whistle. Was it Cuttack? What if it was already Cuttack and he remained locked up inside? He ventured out of the toilet. As he was walking towards the door a man wearing a black coat confronted him, "Ticket?" This must be the T.T.E. Banka could not think any more. The long-bottled up grief and fear erupted with a terrible force. He burst into a howl. God knows what the T.T.E. thought, but he disappeared from the scene leaving him alone. It took a while before his whimpering subsided. Other passengers were eyeing him curiously. Some were asking him his name and were trying to elicit the cause of his outburst. Banka kept on whimpering without bothering to answer. Fortunately, Debashis was not around. He would have ridiculed him for this behaviour. Banka hung his head in shame and kept on silently chanting the Hanuman Chalisa. He thanked Hanuman profusely for saving him from a disaster. Mother had, after all, told the truth. Hanuman alone was the only refuge in times of crisis. And these worthless boys like Debashis? Strange that this fellow played the role of Hanuman when he was a child. He should have played the role of Ravana.

Debashis met him at Cuttack railway station. He was

holding Banka's bag. They got down from the train and walked some distance alongside the track, away from the platform to avoid being checked for a ticket. Banka's bare feet hurt from the sharp stones along the track. But it was easily bearable when he compared it with the great danger he had just escaped.

When they hired a rickshaw, Debashis assured him, "Don't worry, we will pay the rickshaw-puller when we reach home." Debashis had already put his full pants back on by that time. The watch was on his wrist. He had brought out the statue of Radha and Krishna from the bag and was holding it in one hand. Had he really brought this for Pramila? Would Pramila accept his gift? Did she love him too? This fellow was definitely talking big.

But he did really stop the rickshaw a few yards before Pramila's house. Holding the statue in his hand, he advanced towards her two-story building. After he blew a strange kind of whistle a couple of times someone opened the main door of the house. Banka was not able to see the goings-on clearly from a distance and in the faint light. But he was able to make out that a figure collected the statue from Debashis's hand before quickly shutting the door in his face. Whistling the tune of a cinema song gleefully, Debashis returned. Was the figure Pramila? Was it true that Pramila was in love with him? If not, why would she have accepted his gift? Why would she have opened the door so late in the night in response to his whistle?

These questions troubled Banka throughout the night. The attention he received from the members of Debashis's family was like poison to him. The unfamiliar place and the troubling thoughts disturbed his sleep. Even before the day broke he took his bath and set off, wearing Debashis's old pair of slippers.

"Don't you have permission to stay a couple of more days?" asked Debashis

"No, no, I am not feeling well. Please guide me to the bus stop." Banka had completely forgotten Huck and Jim's journey across the river Mississippi.

"Stay back. We will go to a matinee show," Debashis tried to tempt him.

"No, no, I miss my mother very much." He had truly started missing his mother acutely.

"Are you a sissy?" Debashis teased him.

"Will you fetch ten rupees from your mother for me?"

Debashis could sense Banka's anger. He got the entire amount of fifty rupees from his mother and handed it over to Banka. He took out his bicycle and rode towards the OMP Square bus stop with Banka on the carrier. On the way Debashis asked, "Would you like to meet Pramila?"

Banka was on the verge of saying Pramila is a slut, why should I want to meet her? But he restrained himself. He merely shook his head in denial.

Banka breathed a sigh of relief after taking his seat inside the bus. He was happy to have escaped from the clutches of the rascal. He vowed silently not to be taken in by his words ever again. This hypocrite actually went to buy a gift for Pramila, but acted as if he was taking Banka on a trip to Puri. What a great sin it was to go to Puri and not receive the blessings of Lord Jagannath! He silently begged forgiveness from the Lord. The real sinner was Debashis, a liar through and through. So what if he was in love with Pramila! Banka was trying to console himself. But in a corner of his mind he still had a sneaking admiration for Debashis. Debashis might be a thorough schemer, but he certainly had great courage. Did people become bold when they were in love? Were good looks all that was needed for love to flower? Wealth, status, good education, a lucrative job, what about these things? The other thing could be that love begets love. But was there any guarantee that if you loved someone deeply, she would definitely love you back?

These questions continued to haunt Banka all through the bus ride until he reached home.

## ON THE EDGE

*Translated from "Sandigdha Shaishaba"*

"I am Michael."

A fair and handsome young man, over six-feet tall, stretched his palm towards him. Banka was momentarily rattled, not knowing how to act in such a situation.

"I am Banka. I mean Harichandan. Nice to meet you, Sir." Banka shook his hand.

As always, Bajrangbali saved him from another crisis. He had of course read a few books on personality development. But putting theory into practice was another matter. Moreover, he didn't think time for practice would arrive so soon. He was standing alone, leaning against the pillar of the college portico. He had reached college half an hour before the Political Science class, taking advantage of a slight lull in the rain. Half the streets in town were submerged due to the continuous lashing over the last two days. He did not have a raincoat. On the other hand, riding a bicycle, with an unfurled umbrella in one hand, was tough, especially on waterlogged roads. He was in no mood to go to college, but one had to provide a satisfactory explanation for staying home to study. So, when there was a slight respite in the rain he hurried to the college.

The college appeared deserted. There didn't seem to be much activity anywhere. Only peals of laughter were heard at regular intervals from the girls' common room. How did the girls manage to be so happy? Were those bursts of laughter a sign of real happiness? Banka thought over it while parking his cycle in the almost-empty cycle-stand. Just when he was getting out of there was suddenly another spell of rain. Somehow Banka managed to nip across the grassy patch to the portico for shelter. How long had he been standing there alone, leaning against the pillar? It was raining continuously on the tennis courts facing the portico. The force of the rain disturbed the leaves of the deodars, but it had no effect on the hard surface of the tennis courts. Looking at the ridiculous effort of the raindrops to pierce the thick hide of the tennis court, Banka began to wish his mind was as tough as the concrete floor. Then it would not have been disturbed by the peals of laughter emanating from the girls' common room.

"Arrey, why are you calling me Sir? I'm from your class," Michael said while brushing raindrops off his raincoat. Banka, lost in thought, did not notice when Michael had moved so close to him. He was, of course, reassured when he heard him speak in Odia. He had managed his first response in English, but had that young man continued speaking in English what would he have done? He had scored high marks in English in his matriculation examination, but he had not learnt how to have a conversation in English. His English speaking was limited to set speeches in debate competitions.

In the first few days in college he had picked up a few run-of-the-mill expressions like "Nice to meet you", "Thank you", "How are you", etc., from the conversations of the students from English-medium schools. He did not know what language the girls in the common room spoke in, but if you went near, you only heard conversation awash in English.

Even Nandini who had graduated from his own school spoke English loudly when boys were around. She was such a show-off. If she was so adept at speaking English how come she scored such low marks in the matriculation examination, Banka thought to himself. But who could he share his thoughts with? After coming to college Nandini seemed to not recognise Banka. The students who had graduated from Banka's school were studying in various small colleges in villages. None except this Nandini had got a seat in this college. She might not have got a seat either, but her father turned out to be some big officer and managed to get her examination marks enhanced by exercising his influence. In school examinations she was way down in the merit list. Banka and his friends ignored her then. Now at college she did not so much as give him a sideways glance.

Banka had become completely alone in this big college. He was eager to befriend those students from

English-medium schools, but their deportment and manners intimidated him. They always moved around in groups, attired in neatly pressed dresses, shiny shoes, handkerchiefs in their pockets. They appeared to speak English with such finesse that even an Englishman would hang his head in shame. Inside the class the teachers directed questions only at them, paid them all the attention, and even remembered their names. Banka could never marshal enough courage to raise his hand even when he knew the answers to the questions. But how smart the boys from English-medium schools were! They answered all the questions with such promptness! When needed, they would also flirt with girls. Of course, there was another group known for their rowdy ways and they made fun of these boys by calling them daddy-mummy children. Even then Banka wanted to be friends with them. He also wanted to give prompt answers to the teachers' questions and flirt with girls. Would the teachers know his name and....

"From which school did you graduate, Hari?" Michael was asking. They were heading towards the Physics Lecture Theatre through the corridors of the hostel to avoid the rain. Banka didn't understand why the Political Science class was held in the Physics Lecture Theatre. But Michael, addressing him as "Hari", pleased him a lot. In Michael's pronunciation the name sounded like "Harry". If only his name would really have been Harry instead of Banka! As it is, his name was obnoxious, and teachers and friends at school had called him by many ugly nicknames.

The most fair and handsome Mathematics teacher made fun of his dark colour by calling him "monkey". Taking aim at his twisted mouth the Sanskrit pundit called him "Gajanana", after Lord Ganesh, who had the twisted trunk of an elephant for a mouth. For his short height some friends called him "dwarf" and for his plumpness others called him "parbal", a vegetable shaped like a small drum. A few made fun of his innocence by calling him "lotus".

At first, he felt offended by these nicknames. He would burn inside when he heard them. He wanted to tell them to call him by his own name otherwise he would not respond. But how good was his given name? Bankanidhi, bloody hell! In a world full of so many remarkable names, he was given the name Bankanidhi. To ask these bullies to call him by this name was like going from a place where everything was too pricey to one where nothing was available. So he made peace with whatever name they chose to call him. He could not fight with the entire universe. From time to time, though, he would remember the advice of his man-of-letters-cum-mentor Chitta bhai. Chitta bhai had once told him about the Roman orator Cicero. When someone asked him why he had such an ugly name, Cicero answered, "I will leave this name emblazoned on the firmament." Couldn't this name Banka be given a similar fate so that it would shine like a star in the sky?

That was the reason he had studied so sincerely. Mother, of course, had asked him to study well for a different reason, "Son, do well in the examination, otherwise you will not get a seat in a good college."

He was not able to understand why there were only a few seats in good colleges. Such a big college. Couldn't they create a few more seats for the students if they wanted? But he did not want to take any risk. He put all his energy into studying. True to his expectations, he had indeed got a seat in the best college in the state. He had hoped that he would get to stay in a hostel like other students. Money would be sent to him every month by money-order. Saving some money from that he would watch movies with his friends in the cinema halls. He would enjoy paani puri, dahi vada and chaat near Jobra Anicut. He would bring gifts for Nani and Chhotu when he came home during vacations. He would get his hair styled like Amitabh Bachchan's, get clothes stitched in the same cut as Rajesh Khanna at Hind tailor. Whatever he had imagined about his new life in town after meeting his childhood friend Debashis had gone completely awry. First of all, Debashis had failed in the matriculation examination and was unable to set foot in any college. Then, Chacha became the real roadblock; after going through training he had been posted as a policeman in the same town. He suggested that Banka should stay with him and attend college. Father was elated. Banka pleaded before Mother several times, "I shall stay in the hostel, I shall stay in the hostel." But who could contradict Father? Banka did not insist much, preoccupied as he was with his dream of life in a big town and a big college. Moreover, he was eager to somehow get out of home and his old environment.

After coming to town Banka felt that life hadn't changed much. There it was Father's red-eyed angry discipline and here it was Chacha's strict vigil. Being a policeman he was suspicious about every little thing. Each action of his was subjected to at least ten to fifteen minutes of interrogation. "Why did you not go to college today, which holiday is it today, when did you return, where did you go after college, how far have the lessons progressed, have you noted down whatever was taught" and so on. Chacha had cleared his own B.A. examination after three attempts, but asked questions like a Nobel laureate. Added to that his newly-married Chachi would send him to run errands during his study hours. Mother had never asked him to do any chores lest it affected his studies. But this person did not have any such compunctions. On one hand, she made him perform domestic chores and, on the other, she did not care to cook two square meals for him. One day she complained of a headache, on another day of stomach pain or mild fever, she had hundreds of alibis to avoid cooking. On several evenings he had to manage with the roti and tadka Chacha brought from a restaurant. So every night he felt tormented, thinking of Mother's cooking.

What troubled him more than anything else was the environment of the college. Although they addressed him by several disrespectful monikers at school, everyone knew him. Not just the teachers, he was exemplary among the students of the entire school. The story of his success was cited by all, including even the headmaster. Be it class examination or debate competition, regularity or punctuality, he was the undisputed leader. But alas, at college he found that there were equal ranking or even more meritorious students in his class. Not to speak of the principal, even the teachers had no chance of recognising him or remembering his name in the midst of so many students. At school, if you had any doubts regarding your studies the teachers volunteered to clear them. Here, there was nobody even to have a small discussion. At college nobody knew you. You had to make yourself known. Some tried to make their mark by speaking fluent English, some with their flashy outfits, some by speed-riding their rich parents' bikes and cars, and, some by smoking cigarettes and making vulgar remarks at girl students. Banka also thought of a plan to earn a name for himself and set his sights on the upcoming debate competition and literary championship. But when he heard final year M.A. student Srikant bhai's speech, he was completely disheartened. Srikant bhai was planning to contest the students' union election that year. As a part of his preliminary campaign, he came to welcome the freshers. Oh my God! What oratory! His smooth delivery in both Odia and English, interspersed with gentle humour, and his erudition, augmented by supreme self-confidence, stunned Banka into stupefaction. He realised that becoming a literary champion at a mofussil school was one thing, but to even nurse such a dream at this postgraduate college was a completely different proposition.

Then what else was left? How would he pass his college days? Even those days of humiliation were better than not having any identity at all. True, there were occasional thrashings by Father or Mother but at least one could watch movies at the club on Sundays. Mother used to cook special dishes occasionally, and pamper him with extra helpings. Here there was no one to care for him, neither at home nor at college. Chacha was busy in his job and Chachi, bedecked in jewellery, spent most of her time shopping with her sisters.

When you went to college, the English-medium students would not allow anyone into their domain. On the other hand, the students from rural areas were buffoons. They came to the class, their eyes downcast, and went back to their respective holes after classes ended. Banka was scared of the toughies who smoked hemp behind the library, stuffing it inside their cigarettes, made lewd comments at girls standing under the deodar trees, abused the mothers and sisters of whoever incurred their displeasure or wrath and brandished their knives and cycle chains at the drop of a hat. The less said about the girls, the better. They got out of their common room once the bell for the class rang and trudged like geese. They would stand in front of the class till the teacher arrived. Once the teacher entered, they would follow suit and occupy the front benches. After the teacher left, they would again head back to their common room. They would speak so loudly among themselves while walking to and fro that one would think they were the denizens of a seventh heaven. They did not care for the underlings of the world like Banka. It was your supreme fortune if a few English syllables from their mouths reached your ears.

Banka felt he was a denizen, not of the humble earth, but of hell. Wasn't this utter isolation part of what it meant to be consigned to hell? Could one be completely alone in such a big town, such a big college and among the teeming crowd of thousands?

"Arrey, what are you thinking so much about?" The archangel was asking. What name other than archangel could he give him? Michael was the first person in the entire college who had extended a hand of friendship towards him without any precondition.

"No, nothing serious," Banka answered. "I was asking which school you graduated from," Michael said.

Banka told him the name of his school. It was not such a famous school, so he added sheepishly, "An Odia-medium school."

"I know," said Michael without giving much importance to the information.

They had reached the Physics Lecture Theatre. It was strange that, unlike most days, the girls had not gathered in front of the hall. The entire corridor looked empty. When they entered the hall only five or six of the English-medium students were present. The electric bulbs were shining brightly, three or four ceiling fans were revolving, emitting an ugly mechanical whirr. The wings of all the other fans had been twisted into lotus shapes by miscreants. "Chakuludu Elpo" was written in big, bold, beautiful Odia letters on the blackboard.

Banka remembered that the students from the back benches had recently started addressing the Political Science lecturer by this name. The teacher had a strong southern accent, and his style of teaching was rather odd. These smart boys harassed him by shouting "Chakuludu Elpo" loudly again and again from the back benches. Banka asked the Telugu domestic help who cleaned the utensils at Chacha's place the meaning of the phrase. When he learnt that the phrase meant "washerman, go back", their actions seemed very cruel to him. A teacher may be unable to teach well, but perhaps with more experience, he would be able to teach well someday. But to cast aspersions on one's caste or religion, whatever be one's inability, was rude in the extreme. They were not even content with that. They had gone ahead and written those words on the blackboard in bold letters. Banka had gained a lot of self-confidence after having a conversation with Michael. When Michael went over and joined his group of English-medium school boys, he tore a piece of paper from his notebook, walked over to the blackboard and began rubbing off the letters.

It took a while for the boys to comprehend what Banka was up to.

"What are you doing there?" The most hefty-looking fellow asked him loudly.

He was the son of the police IG or DIG. Sometimes

he came to college in a car with a yellow lamp mounted on it. A senior student had once tried to rag him and had ended up in the police station. On top of that, he was fined twenty-five rupees by the principal.

"I am wiping off this vulgar comment," Banka answered.

"From which angle does it appear vulgar to you?" The hefty Debadutta Panda spoke in a challenging tone.

"Casting aspersions on a teacher's caste, is it not vulgar?" Banka felt a surge of courage within him.

"Has Ananda Rao taken leave today and sent you to teach his class?" The whole group laughed heartily at this comment. Mustering all his courage, Banka answered in English, "Civic sense is a part of learning political science."

"Arrey, hear hear, he is speaking wonderful English, this offspring of Gandhi. Michael, where did you locate this phenomenon?" Then in downright filthy language he made such nasty remarks involving Banka's mother that his face reddened from shame and humiliation. In great anger he shouted, "Shut up, you bastard."

Everyone was stunned for a while. Then the whole group charged towards Banka. "What do you mean by calling him a bastard?" They attacked in unison.

Michael of course was trying to restrain them vainly, "Hey, leave him alone."

Without heeding his words they lifted Banka bodily and carried him towards the lawn. One of the cheap plastic chappals Chacha had given him to wear during the rainy season slipped off his foot. In a moment he found himself lying on the lawn full of water and slush.

Although he was not hurt, he lay there for some time, not knowing what to do till the group of English-medium boys left. More than the behaviour of Debadutta and the other boys, he was pained by what Michael did. Although Banka was still lying in the slush he chose to walk away with his group. The feeling of courage that had surged in him on befriending Michael seemed to have been washed away by the water and slush on the lawn. In its place simmered a futile anger and helplessness. After lifting himself up from the lawn Banka sat leaning against a pillar on the veranda. He asked himself why he was so ill-fated. In the newspaper he read regularly about rapes, murders, street fights, and pillage. Those criminals were able to live in this world with their heads held high; but why was a God-fearing good student like him so oppressed, at home, outside home, almost everywhere? He tried to think as far back as he could. No, he had not committed any crime for which he had to suffer such ignominy throughout his life. At home he suffered at the hands of Father, Mother, uncle, auntie and other relatives. Outside of home friends, teachers and even toughies and bullies tormented him. Some human beings were perhaps destined to suffer. Even if they were on the right path they tripped and slipped and stumbled again and again. They had no respite anywhere.

"Hey, it has already been declared a rainy day and you are sitting here alone? Are you okay?"

Banka looked up and saw Guman Singh, the leader of the toughies. Banka was scared at first; Guman Singh's appearance would inspire fear in anyone. Black like charcoal, he sported thick curly hair on his head and a thick steel ring was wrapped around his wrist. In sharp contrast to his colour there was a vermilion mark on his forehead. He was five to six years senior to his classmates in age. He had flunked his matriculation examination many times. That year he was able to do so by resorting to cheating at an examination centre in a remote village. Not only that, he scored such high marks that he was able to get a seat in such a prestigious college. He rarely attended classes. Forget the students, even the teachers were afraid of him. He was notorious and, besides, he belonged to the most notorious area in town.

"It has been declared a holiday, don't you know?" Guman Singh asked again. "Principal's discussionary holiday." He mixed up "discretionary" with "discussionary".

"Is there a problem? Where do you live? If you want I can drop you there," Guman Singh assured him.

"No, I have my cycle," Banka answered hurriedly. If Guman went to his house and Chacha got to learn about it, all hell would break loose.

"Was there some skirmish with those daddy-mummy children?'"

"No, nothing." Banka did not want his humiliation made public. Apart from that, should he share his secret grief with a creature like Guman Singh? At the same time he was not able to think of anyone in this whole wide world to whom he could unburden his sorrow. He could have shared this with Pramila perhaps, or Debashis. But both had been lost to him exactly like his childhood.

"Brother, don't be so secretive with us. Tell us frankly what happened. We will take revenge. The speed with which they left from here, we thought something unpleasant has taken place. That is why we came here. Now we see you are covered with mud. Tell us, don't be scared."

As he spoke, Guman Singh seemed to be imitating the mannerisms of the Odia film hero Sriram Panda. But his language came straight from the slums of Cuttack. Despite the recent incident of humiliation Banka felt like laughing at his words. But he reckoned he could get rid of Guman by telling him a lie. But the pair of plastic chappals... all his anger was now concentrated on Chacha. He had wanted to buy a pair of shoes from a Bata showroom as soon as he was admitted to college. Mother, too, went along with it. Like with everything else, Father threw cold water on the project. He recited a Sanskrit shloka, which meant a fool, draped in good attire, looked fine from a distance, but once he opened his mouth his idiocy was advertised for the entire world. As if anything uttered in Sanskrit became a hundred per cent truth. Had Mother exerted herself his shoes would have been bought. But like a sycophant, Chacha broke in saying that leather shoes would be spoiled in the rain; there would be more sense in buying full shoes in the winter. So, Banka had to manage with a pair of cheap plastic chappals. Had he been wearing full shoes, Banka could have landed a kick on the chest of each one of them when they lifted him up in the air. But alas, when he swung his legs the first thing that slipped off his feet was those chappals.

Cursing his uncle silently for the misfortune, Banka gathered his mud-smeared chappals and said, "Those bastards threw me on the lawn."

"How dare they? Did they throw you for no reason? What did you do?" asked Guman. "They were foul-mouthing you and your friends. I threatened to spill the beans before you." He himself was surprised on spawning such a lie.

"Wait, you sons-of-bitches. Being thread they are rubbing themselves against the edge of a sword. They will be cut in two. I said things in a roundabout way." Guman Singh boasted in a theatrical manner. "We will settle the score."

The rain had subsided. They walked towards the cycle stand. "In which area do you live?" asked Guman.

Banka told him the name of the locality where they lived in a rented house. "Come, let us accompany you to your area. We have to go past it."

Grabbing their bicycles they went past the college campus. There was a posh stationery shop across the college gate. The boys from rich families frequented that shop for coffee. There was an automatic coffee vending machine with a spout, beneath which you had to hold your cup, and push the button for the coffee to come out.

Banka was tempted to have some coffee there sometimes. But he was not allowed enough pocket money to indulge in that luxury. Whatever little money he got was spent on maintaining the bicycle. "Look, they are drinking coffee." Banka pointed at the stationery shop. Debadutta, Michael and their friends were drinking coffee and smoking cigarettes. They had not seen either Banka or Guman Singh, so engrossed they were in themselves.

"It's that fatso, that petrol-tank, the son of DIG Panda? One day I am going to teach that rascal a harsh lesson. Let the students union election end, I will paint his snout red. A river of blood will flow."

They were riding their cycles in the direction of Banka's house. But he was not happy with Guman Singh's vow of revenge. He realised that Guman Singh had taken admission in the college only to contest the election. A couple of times he had noticed Guman and his gang of ruffians pasting leaflets of a political party on the walls of the college. His suspicion was confirmed after Guman's admission. Maybe he was showing sympathy now to get Banka's vote during the election.

"How many students are there from your locality in our college?" Guman was asking.

Banka's spirit had withered. The brief excitement he had felt after noticing Debadutta and his friends had subsided.

"I don't know," he answered.

"Try to find out within a week," Guman said.

"Yes," Banka responded without any enthusiasm.

Throughout the ride Guman went on talking about how he would line up a connection with the Chief Minister once he was elected as the Secretary of the Students' Union, how he would use his clout to throw the English-medium students out of the college and so on. Banka was not paying attention. He thought to himself, the union election was an annual affair. Guman would need the votes of Debadutta and his friends to win the election, this year and next year as well. Even if he was defeated, he would have hopes of winning next time. Once he was trapped in the temptation of an election victory, how could he take revenge? No one with political ambitions, therefore, was ever helpful to ordinary students like him.

They had reached Banka's house. The rain had completely stopped now. For some reason Chacha, instead of being at the office, was standing on the veranda of the house.

"Is this your house? Who is that man?" Guman Singh whispered.

"He is my uncle." Guman Singh cycled away, swift as lightning, before Banka could answer.

Before Banka could lean his cycle against the stand, Chacha's bawling came. "Where were you roaming around with that rascal? Why are your pants and shirt smeared with mud? Where did you do your mischief mongering? Why were you at college when it is closed due to rain?"

For a long time there had been no attack on him at home because of his excellent result in the matriculation examination. So Banka was taken aback by Chacha's erupting like a volcano. "He studies in our class," he somehow managed to explain.

A sound slap fell on his cheek. "Studies in your class? He is a rogue, a black-marketeer. I have picked him up from the cinema hall several times and thrashed him inside the police station. And you are saying he studies in your class. What does he study? Tell me the truth, where were you roaming with him?"

Banka's face turned red from the police slap. There was of course no river of blood, but the inside of his mouth tasted salty with fresh blood. The base of the ear started to hum and buzz. Like every time, he felt like crying, but he restrained himself with great difficulty. He wiped the tears running down his cheeks with the back of his palm. His body was shaking in anger from repressing his cry.

He wanted to ask Chacha why he was asking him these questions. Why didn't he ask who awarded Guman Singh such high marks, which enabled him to go to such a prestigious college? Why was he not asking the principal who had provided him a seat in the college? Why didn't he question the Chief Minister who, as the president of his party, had chosen Guman as a candidate for the post of Secretary of the Students' Union? Why didn't he challenge his own DIG Panda, whose son, protected by his father's clout, called teachers names and ragged innocent students?

Banka knew Chacha did not have that kind of

courage. He might not have answers to his questions. Did a man become courageous just by wearing a khaki dress? Guman Singh had at least promised to draw a river of blood from the bodies of Debadutta and his friends after the election. Could Chacha give such an assurance, risking his job?

At last, surprising even himself, Banka announced his decision in a grave voice, "I will stay in the hostel and study."

Chacha bore down on him at these words, "What did you say, what did you say? Bloody rogue. A slip of a boy, does not even know how to wipe his own bottom. Roaming around with cinema ticket black-marketeers. Talking back when asked to explain."

There might have been more thrashing but Chachi came running out of the house when she heard Chacha yelling.

"Hey, why are you hitting him? He is not your own child. I have been warning you from the beginning. You are nurturing a viper in your bosom. Sons are not performing the last rites of their own parents these days, and you are expecting the sons of others to be loyal to you? Send word to your brother. Let him take his son and leave him in a hostel."

"Shut up, you obnoxious woman. Go back inside. Who asked you to barge in?" All Uncle's anger was now concentrated on his wife. He shouted with such force that she was literally pushed back into the house.

"Yes, send word to Father. I will stay in a hostel

or a mess. I will not stay here another minute," Banka said this with such firmness that Chacha was completely stunned. He kept looking blankly at Banka. Without batting an eyelid Banka, too, stared back at his uncle. He felt as if all of time and even the earth stood still. He had perhaps found answers to all the questions that had plagued him throughout his childhood. Questions such as why he was thrashed if somebody wrote a love letter to the neighbour's daughter, if Chacha flunked his examination, if Father came back home after being told off by his superior officer, if Mother quarrelled with his grandmother. He was now free of all his guilt and doubt.

In the clarity of that moment he realised that his misfortune would not end even if Father turned up. He might have to face a bigger crisis. He might be completely alone then. His uncle and auntie, father and mother, sister, Chhotu, his brother, Debadutta, Michael, the students of the English-medium school, would be ranged against him. Even Guman Singh, who boasted that he would draw blood from the body of DIG Panda's son, but ran away in fear when he saw a lowly police sub-inspector, might not be of any use to him. Would Bajrangbali, his companion during all his lonely and frightful moments, be able to deliver him from this hell of aloneness? Perhaps not. But he still felt a strong wave of resolution welling up inside him. If this hell was his fate, his ultimate destiny, then he would delve deep into its bottomless pit, fully conscious. An endless fall into that hell was far better than the deceptions involved in keeping up appearances.

Banka went into his room, walking past Chacha who stood frozen on the veranda, unable to decide what to do. After changing his dirty clothes, he set about packing his clothes and books.

ACKNOWLEDGEMENTS

Author

I am grateful to Manu Dash, poet and publisher, Sailendra Narayan Tripathy, academic and poet, and my friends Nilekha and Umesh, for planting in me the idea of an English version of *Banka Harichandan*.

Translator

The Odia original of *The Life and Times of Banka Harichandan* is a unique and groundbreaking work of serious literary exploration centred on the child. No such sustained and book length coming-of-age narrative that is delivered through a sequence of discrete tales exists in modern Odia letters or, I suspect, in the contemporary regional language corpus in India. That the author, Dipti Ranjan Pattanaik, chose me as the mediator for the English version of this book makes me feel honoured. My gratitude increases several-fold when I recall the extent of the author's involvement with the translation that makes him my collaborator.

This translation was undertaken during the protracted period of isolation, fear and ennui bred by a long-reigning pandemic. With book production work stalled, and, with publishers deluged with huge backlogs, the manuscript seemed fated to wilt and die before seeing the light of day. At this point a timely tip from Ananya Bhatia, formerly Commissioning Editor, OUP and Penguin, was like a ray of bright light in the prevailing darkness. A big 'thank you' to Ananya for showing the way that led to the door of Arpita Das of Yoda Press.

And, of course, thanks galore to Arpita for giving Banka Harichandan a secure and caring home. It is also her and Ishita Gupta, Commissioning Editor at Yoda Press, who deserve my grateful and sincere approbation for the reinforcement of that love and security through a significant tie-up with Simon & Schuster, India. Banka Harichandan can now boast of double parentage in a single home.

The same double privilege came Banka Harichandan's way in the form of two heart-warming endorsements from Paul Zacharia and Chandrahas Choudhury. I cannot thank them enough.

Last but not least, I owe a special word of thanks to my wife Swarnarenu for her continued support and assurances.

## ABOUT THE AUTHOR AND TRANSLATOR

**Dipti R. Pattanaik** teaches English at Banaras Hindu University, Varanasi. He is a bilingual writer, literary critic and translator. He writes short stories and essays on literary criticism both in Odia and English. His essays and short stories have appeared in major journals in India and abroad. His translations, from English to Odia and Odia to English, have been published by major publishers. He has received the Odisha Sahitya Akademi Award, National Katha Award and Jhankara Award, among others, for his creative writing, and the Fakir Mohan Sahityashree Award for his translation.

**Himansu S. Mohapatra** is a former Professor of English, Utkal University. He has produced, with Paul St-Pierre, an edited volume of Odia stories in English translation, entitled *The Other Side of Reason* (2008), and, three books of translation: *Following My Heart* (2023), an autobiographical work by J.M. Joarda, *Battles of Our Own* (2022), an 'industrial novel' set in Odisha, by Jagadish Mohanty, and *Basanti: Writing the New Woman* (2019), the first woman-oriented Odia novel, written by nine authors in 1931. A selection of his literary journalism has been published as *Model of the Middle* (2014). He studied at Sambalpur University, Odisha and University of East Anglia, UK. He is currently Visiting Professor of English at Central University of Odisha, Koraput.